Advance praise

"There is only one New Mexico! And there's only one Martha Egan. Híjole, her book, *La Ranfla and Other New Mexico Stories*, is full of wild magic and the unconquered, unvanquished human spirit that will foster in all its readers a love for a place that is still the Wild West. Only someone who knows los ins y los outs can tell this story. Órale, Comadrita, the ride is really good."

DENISE CHÁVEZ
author of *A Taco Testimony: Meditations on Family, Food, and Culture*

"In *La Ranfla*, Martha Egan captures the quirkiness of Northern New Mexico in a series of colorfully drawn short stories rich with wonderfully authentic characters. It's a fine, fine ride."

ANNE HILLERMAN
author of *Santa Fe Flavors* and *Hillerman's Landscape: On the Road with an American Legend*

"The literary equivalent of a green chile fix, this collection of Martha Egan's is just as addicting—a liberal serving of what it feels like to live in New Mexico—the Land of Entrapment—especially as a gringa."

CHRISTINE MATHER
author of *Christine Mather's Santa Fe Christmas*

rave reviews for other novels by Martha Egan

"Has Carl Hiaasen switched states and gender or what??? Is the best-selling mystery novelist now targeting his noir satires not at Florida but New Mexico, going undercover as a Santa Fe gallery owner named Martha Egan? Egan's *Clearing Customs* wages jihad on the same brand of self-serving cretins that overpopulate Hiaasen's Miami, heavy-handed, power hungry, sloppy politicos and so-called public servants too ready to break the law to enforce it. And anybody who loves Hiaasen will have a ball reading Egan's fast-paced, chile-flavored, and always entertaining mystery."

BOB SHACOCHIS
American Book Award, 1985, *Easy in the Islands*;
Prix de Rome, 1989, *The Next New World*

"If you suspected the government was tapping your phone, following you around, and otherwise harassing you unjustly, you could passively ascribe it all to paranoia, or, like Beverly Parmentier, the protagonist in this exciting novel, you could fight back. I'd bet that, in a similar situation, the author, Martha Egan, would do just what Beverly Parmentier did and that she'd be as successful at it as she is in the writing of this terrific and engaging story."

FRED HARRIS
former US Senator (D-OK),
author of ten nonfiction books and three novels

"*Coyota* is the consummate Southwestern novel, a story of the peaceful Mexicos, new and old, and the underbelly of corruption that lies beneath them. . . . Smart, feisty, vulnerable Nena Herrera-Casey, an innocent and principled bystander . . . is swept onto the vicious trading field where honest commerce with Mexico and drug trafficking collide. Egan tells her story with the sure hand of a writer who knows both sides of the peso."

SARA VOORHEES
Author of *The Lumière Affair: A Novel of Cannes*

"Egan's descriptive writing is vivid and compelling."

DAVID STEINBERG
The Albuquerque Journal

"A gripping thriller all the way through."

Midwest Book Review

"It is apparent that author Martha Egan, who is an importer herself, is very familiar with Mexico and its culture and the Hispanic culture of the Southwest, of which she writes without sentimentality or clichés. *Coyota* is highly recommended for its vividness and well-crafted plot."

ADRIAN BUSTAMANTE
La Herencia

La Ranfla & Other New Mexico Stories

Also by Martha Egan

La Ranfla

& other
New Mexico stories

martha egan

Papalote Press

Santa Fe

Were I to be a story thief, shamelessly pilfering snippets of other people's true life tales and weaving them into a fabric of fiction they might or might not recognize, I would mean no offense, and would hope none be taken. But I would never admit to such theft. In like manner, if some of the places that occurred to me in my mental musings and hypnagogic states did actually exist outside of my imagined world, it would be mere happenstance.

©2009 Papalote Press

Papalote Press
P.O. Box 32058
Santa Fe NM 87594
www.papalotepress.com

ISBN 978-0-9755881-4-7 cloth
Library of Congress Control Number: 2009906431

FIRST PRINTING
This book is printed on acid-free, archival quality paper.
Manufactured in the USA.

9 8 7 6 5 4 3 2 1

For New Mexico, my chosen home—
its dramatic landscapes, its sky,
and most of all, its people.

But what's an honest soul to do? I don't know. I can say: be loyal to what you love, be true to the Earth, fight your enemies with passion and laughter; but what does this mean? It's a formula too general to be useful, an intuition too personal to be generally acceptable. So there you are.

Edward Abbey

CONTENTS

1
La Ranfla

PART I The Lesabre

Mary Louise Kowalski bumped open the door to the Safeway with her hip and emerged into the California sunshine carrying a brown paper sack of groceries. Strands of her long, red hair floated behind her like streamers in the steady breeze coming inland from San Francisco Bay. In the top of her bag rode a heaping pint of ripe strawberries with an irresistibly sweet scent. She popped one into her mouth and tossed the hull over her shoulder. Sustenance for the long walk to her apartment.

A little girl sitting on the curb held up a whimpering, scrawny puppy with a distended belly. "Look, lady! He's only a dollar!" she pleaded.

Mary Louise felt sorry for the puppy and the girl, but the last thing she needed was a dog.

"Hey, baby! Want a ride?" shouted a tubby, middle-aged man cruising by in a red Mustang convertible. When she paid him no mind, he gunned his engine and screeched away.

Farther down the street, a covey of Hare Krishnas gathered where someone had written "WAR" in drippy, white paint under the "STOP" on a stop sign. Their heads bald, their faces blank with bliss, they tinkled finger cymbals and rattled tambourines. One of them aggressively peddled incense while his colleagues swayed in saffron-colored robes and chanted mindlessly. Mary Louise strode through them.

A teenager with limp, stringy hair to his shoulders was waiting for her on the sidewalk. He whispered as she walked past: "Wanna score a lid? It's dynamite weed."

"This is getting tiresome," Mary Louise thought. "I'm accosted every five feet."

Then a tall, sturdy young man crossed the street and swung into step beside her. Before he could say anything, she barked at him: "No, I don't have any spare change!"

He stepped back in exaggerated alarm. "Well, that makes two of us," he said. "Need a hand with those groceries?" He helped himself to a strawberry.

Mary Louise kept going, looking straight ahead, the bag clutched to her chest. The best way to deal with these pesky street people was to ignore them.

He trotted around, facing her, and began to walk backward. "I don't take no for an answer, y'know." He smiled and tossed another berry into his mouth, hull and all.

She maintained a frosty silence.

"How about a cuppa java?" he said jovially. "You look like you could use perkin' up—no pun intended—and I'm buyin'. My name's Oso—it means bear." He threw his arms into the air. In a deep, thundering voice, he growled at her. "GrrrrrrrrrRRRRR."

Mary Louise almost dropped her bag.

"Oops. I didn't mean to scare you," Oso said. "I'm actually harmless. Honest."

She appraised him. He was sort of bearlike—more than six feet tall, broad shouldered, big boned, but light on his feet. His kinky, neatly trimmed, bright orange beard reminded her of a copper scouring pad. The tie-dyed, rainbow colored T-shirt he wore was clean. So were his jeans, perhaps the only pair in Berkeley without patches. A pink bandanna tied around his forehead held his abundant, wavy, brown hair back from his face and gave him a jaunty air. He looked OK. Actually, Mary Louise thought, noting the twinkle in his Windex blue eyes, he looked better than OK.

"Uh, oh," Oso said. "For a second there, I thought I saw a smile. A teensy-weensy smile."

"Look," Mary Louise said to herself, "agreeing to have coffee with this guy isn't like inviting Charlie Manson into my boudoir." Besides, she didn't intend to devote the rest of such a balmy afternoon to her law books. She handed him the bag of groceries.

"OK," she said, "but leave me a few strawberries, will ya?"

They walked around the corner to a small Mexican restaurant and sat at an outside table. "I heartily recommend the churros and hot chocolate," Oso said. "What'll you have?"

"What are churros?" she asked.

"Linear doughnuts, mighty tasty."

"Sure, I'll try them."

When the waiter came, Oso ordered in what sounded to Mary Louise like fluent Spanish. In minutes, the man was back with their food. He chatted with Oso for a bit, picked up his tray, and went back inside.

"Your Spanish sounds authentic. Did you study it in school?" Mary Louise asked.

"Not at first. I dropped out of high school for a year and picked oranges down south with the mojados. Wonderful people. They're the ones who named me Oso. 'Thackeray' was too much for them. They taught me orchard Spanish. I learned the polite language when I went back to school. I already had a huge vocabulary of cuss words."

"Are you a student?" Mary Louise asked.

"Not here. My parents live in Marin. I'm in town to convince my draft board I'm seriously whacko. I dropped a little acid before I went to see them the other day and scared the bejesus out of them patriots."

"So are they going to give you a deferment?"

"I sure as hell hope not. I'm going for a full-fledged 4-F. I'm out to convince those warmongering sonsa bitches I'm a raving paranoid schizophrenic kleptomaniac pervert with flatulence, vertigo, incontinence, shingles, halitosis, and terminal athlete's foot."

"My God. Do you actually have any of those things?"

"Naw, but I wore my mother's black bra under a see-through blouse for the interview. That wowed 'em."

Mary Louise giggled.

"How about you?" he asked.

"I'm a first-year law student. Boring, huh?"

"Not at all. How's it going?"

"I've got a ton of reading, but I'm excited. I'd like to do poverty law after I get my degree."

"From what I hear, then you, too, will join the ranks of the impecunious. Did you do your undergrad work at Berkeley?"

"No. I went to UW/Madison, mostly because I got a Governor's Scholarship."

"Ah, so you're from Wisconsin."

"Yeah, a little town near Milwaukee called Cedarburg. One of those peaceful, predictable, wholesome places where everybody knows everybody, and nothing much ever changes. Berkeley is quite an eye opener."

"Even after Madison?"

"Things were certainly hot there with the constant anti-war protests. Don't get me wrong—I'm as much against the war as anyone. But this place can be a little overwhelming."

"I can dig it," Oso said. "For a comely redhead like you, merely walking down the street is probably like running a gauntlet."

Mary Louise blushed in spite of herself.

"My campus is every bit as weird."

"Where's that?"

"Cambridge."

"In England?"

"Nope. Cambridge, Mass. I'm working on a doctorate in plant physiology at Harvard."

"Really?" Mary Louise wondered. "Is this man I took for another hippie/dropout/panhandler a Harvard-educated botanist?" She was skeptical.

"So what's your dissertation on?" She rested her chin on her fist.

"You don't believe me, do you?" he said wryly. "How's this? *Characterization of proteinases and the role of light in the inductive secretions of the Drosera roraimae of the Venezuelan Roraima Tepui.* Sound plausible?"

"Yeah," she said, although she wasn't convinced. Maybe he went to the library to look up something sufficiently pedantic.

"The Drosera's a carnivorous plant, kinda spiky and sticky. It eats bugs."

"Cool!" she said.

Mary Louise took back her groceries and walked home alone. She didn't want Oso to know where she lived. He seemed acceptable, but she was a small town girl, programmed to be cautious, especially with a man she'd met on the street. Then again, she did give him her phone number. They planned to meet on the weekend for a walk around campus. "That's probably safe enough," she thought.

Mary Louise and Oso began seeing a lot of each other. She had never met anyone like him. He was brilliant. He had read everything imaginable. He was unselfconscious, wildly spontaneous, with a devil-may-care attitude and a funny, folksy way of talking. She noticed he dropped the endings of his verbs like a hillbilly, but peppered his sentences with twenty-dollar words.

"I guess it's my half-assed way of compensating for being the progeny of university professors," he said. "Pathetic, ain't it?"

Mary Louise could talk to him about anything, including her frustrations with law school. Most important, he made her laugh harder than she'd ever laughed before, until her face hurt. In bed, he was a dynamo.

He loved to drive her big, yellow 1961 Buick LeSabre.

"Her name's Janet," Mary Louise explained. "I named her after my grandmother. She gave her to me."

"This broad's got class," he said. "Big and sleek as a racehorse. Now compare her to an AMC Gremlin."

"A Gremlin probably gets much better gas mileage."

"For sure. My mom says that's why she bought one. The day they came out—last April Fool's Day."

On weekends, they drove "Buster," Oso's green and orange Volkswagen camper bus with its VW insignia on the front that had been converted into a peace sign. They camped out on beaches, or they headed for prime hiking spots: Point Reyes, Yosemite, Muir Woods.

Mary Louise fell hard for Oso. Even while she was reading her law books, recollections of funny things he'd said intervened in her every synapse as if borne on a radio signal that wouldn't quit. He was jamming her brain.

As they lay in bed curled into each other one night, pleasantly exhausted and sweaty after making love, Mary Louise thought: "God, I hope we've got a future together." She lazily twined her fingers in his springy chest hair, screwed up her courage, and said: "Oso, do you have a plan?"

"Yup. I got word from my draft board today."

He took note of her panic-stricken face and kissed her gently on her forehead. "Hang loose, Sweet Pea. No, I'm not headed for Nam. I didn't get the 4-F, but they did give me another eighteen months on my student deferment. I'm packing up Buster next week and heading for northern New Mexico."

Her heart felt like it was weighted with wet cement. "New Mexico? What are you going to do there?"

"I'm fixin' to work on my dissertation while contemplating the various shades of red in the sunsets on the Sangre de Cristo Mountains under the influence of some really spectacular dope I plan to grow. Put those many years of studyin' plants to good use." He chucked her under the chin. "You're coming to see me after the semester ends, aren'cha, Sweet Pea?"

Once Oso left for New Mexico, Mary Louise realized how disillusioned she was with law school. It was a different place without him to cheer her on. The other students were competitive to the point of hostility, even the other women, who usually sat together in a clutch toward the back of the auditorium. Although she enjoyed her courses and the intellectual challenge, she was confused by the rhetoric.

"Isn't the point of the American legal system justice?" she asked Dick Duckworth, the professor conducting her torts class.

"Young lady," he scoffed. "Get real. The point of the law is The Law. The argument. If you can't get your head wrapped around that, you should go home, get married, and have babies."

The entire auditorium of a hundred mostly white male students burst out laughing.

The professor continued to bully her in nearly every class. "Do you really think you can use the legal system for social change? How naïve can you get?"

She went to her adviser, Dr. Bregman, to complain about Duckworth. To her surprise and dismay, he wasn't supportive.

"Miss Kowalski, you have to get used to being a minority," he said. "Most attorneys aren't sure women are suited to the law, you know, and they don't want to work with you girls. You're too emotional, too conciliatory, too easy to push around. More than anything, you won't fit into the male culture of a law practice. You'll have a hard time getting a job when you finish—if you finish."

Oso called shortly after he settled into Los Llanos, a village in northern New Mexico. Mary Louise was close to tears. "I am so miserable. This place is a drag without you."

"I miss you, too, Sweet Pea. I miss you more than you can imagine. I can't wait for summer to come. In fact, I was so lonesome on the trip to New Mexico, I picked up a dog while I was driving through Indian Country. Or rather, he picked me up. I stopped for gas and rolling papers at the Circle K in Tuba City and came out to find this nasty looking, flea-bitten, part Chow mutt sitting in the driver's seat of my Buster like he owned the place. I asked around, and everybody said he was a stray as far as they knew. I named him Rez Dog. He's a special pal, but you're much better looking. Thing is, though, he comes when I call him."

Oso and Mary Louise wrote each other long, passionate, funny letters. Now and then, they talked on the phone, mostly late at night when calls were cheap.

Mary Louise did her best to concentrate on her studies. But the morning the torts prof threw yet one more public jibe at her in class, she leaped to her feet and exploded. "Listen, you misogynistic sack of shit. What makes you think you're such hot stuff? You're never prepared for class. You can't answer half our questions. Where did you get your law degree? In a box of Cracker Jacks? The rest of you guys are dickheads, too, laughing at his appalling sexist jokes. And you *girls,* don't you have any self-respect? Tell this jackass to go fuck himself."

Even at Berkeley, chins hit the floor.

Mary Louise sold her law texts back to the bookstore that very afternoon, packed her few possessions into Janet, and headed for New Mexico.

Before Oso left Berkeley, he had rolled her a dozen fat joints. "It's the best dope I've ever grown; ergo it's the best dope you've ever smoked!" he promised. Little did he know that she'd never smoked so much as a cigarette until she met him.

The thick doobies she puffed as she cruised down the road heading southeast induced a carefree mood of dreamy optimism. By the time she crossed the California-Arizona border, she had tossed her wholesome, Midwestern, magna cum laude, good-girl persona out the window like a used Kleenex. By the time she reached the Arizona-New Mexico border, inspired by the zillions of sparkling stars lighting up the black desert night, Mary Louise Kowalski had rechristened herself Starshine. She changed her car's name, too. Janet became Janis, after her favorite singer.

By the second day of their new incarnation, Janis began to make funny noises that sounded more serious to Starshine than the rattle of pebbles in the car's hubcaps or the growling rumble escaping the pinholes in her salt-rusted tailpipe. She did her best not to panic, but her joyful mood crashed like a spent bottle rocket. No longer was she a blithe spirit floating through a magic land of endless blue sky and sunlight. Suddenly, she was a woman alone driving an iffy, aged car across an empty landscape as alien to her as the moon. When she considered the possibility that Janis might break down in the middle of nowhere, she freaked out. "Shit!" she said aloud, pounding the steering wheel. "Don't let me down now. Please. Please. I'll get you checked out as soon as I can."

Starshine turned into the first service station she came to, a two-pump Mobil Oil in the nearest town, Española, New Mexico. A pair of rail-thin teenagers—brothers, she thought—sauntered out of a dilapidated wood plank and adobe brick garage that looked like it was held together with discarded license plates. They were a little rough looking, but then, so were garage guys everywhere, Starshine reminded herself.

She sat still behind the steering wheel as the boys approached her car, hoping she looked calm and collected.

One of the teenagers swiped at her bug-splattered windshield with a dirty rag, while the other walked up to her open window and leaned in. Starshine tensed. Exhaling stale cigarette breath and staring down her dress, he asked her if she wanted regular, extra, or premium, adding after a pause, "We don't got nothin' but reg'lar."

As casually as possible, she said: "Actually, I was hoping you could help me figure out a weird noise coming from the engine. But you might as well put some gas in, too. Regular's OK."

The Ragman began to fill the tank. "Eeeee, I like your ranfla, lady," he said, running his grease-blackened hands over the Buick's three vents and chromed grill.

"My what?" Starshine asked nervously. New Mexicans had a funny, singsong way of talking. Half the time, she had no idea what they were saying. Was he admiring her boobs? Her lime green sunglasses? The pink and orange, flower patterned, too short shift riding up her thighs?

"Your ranfla—your ride."

"My ride? Oh, you mean my car." she said, relieved at deciphering his unfamiliar lingo. "Yeah, my grandmother gave it to me for graduation."

"Let's see what you got," the Ragman said, unlatching the hood.

The brothers muttered to each other in a musical mixture of Spanish and English, and admired the large Dynaflow engine filling the car's front-end cavity with grimy, formidable metal. They checked the oil. "You're down a quart, lady," one said.

"I'm not surprised. But I don't think that's the problem. Let me start her up."

The car roared to life. The boys leaped back with respect and then inched closer. Tipping their heads, they listened to the clanking that shook the LeSabre's entire body.

"Better go get Abuelito," the Ragman said to his brother.

Starshine was clueless. Did that mean motor oil?

The brother disappeared into the garage and reappeared, followed by a wizened, whiskered codger who wiped his hands on the sides of his oil-spattered jumpsuit, tottering from one stiff leg to the other as he came up to the car. "¿Qué tiene?" he asked in a croaky voice.

"No sabemos," the boys said in unison.

He listened to the engine for a while, grunted, and then slowly ambled back into the garage. When he returned, Starshine noted with alarm that he was carrying a crowbar. "Holy shit," she thought. "Now what? Ohhh, why did I ever leave Berkeley?"

The old man ignored her. Leaning under the hood, he put the straight end of the crowbar against the engine block and held the curved end to his ear. After listening carefully for a while, he mumbled something in Spanish.

The Ragman interpreted for her. "Abuelito says you gonna throw a rod."

Starshine gave him a blank look. "What's that mean?"

"Lady, your engine's gonna blow up."

His brother chimed in: "Yeah, but maybe not right away."

"I only need to make it to Los Llanos," she said, trying not to whine. "Is it far?"

"Maybe another sixty miles or so," the Ragman said. "I'll ask Abuelito what he thinks."

The boys conferred with their grandfather. "Yeah, you can probably get that far," the younger one said. "But take it easy, especially going up them hills."

Starshine drove into the yard where Oso stood under the portal of a rundown adobe house set in a field of silver and white chamisa bushes and last fall's dried sunflowers. He held the collar of the big, furry, black dog barking furiously at her.

"What took ya so long?" he hollered. He jumped off the porch, loped up to her, and wrapped her in his thick arms.

"You were expecting me?" Starshine asked, looking up into his glacier blue eyes. "I thought you'd be surprised. I wasn't planning on coming until after the semester was over."

"Nope," he said. "I knew you had it bad for me and Mr. Willy. Whaddaya say we find out if he remembers you?"

In fair weather, Starshine and Oso readied the field behind the house for planting. They mended fences and dug out irrigation ditches choked with tumbleweeds. If it was too hot, too chilly, or too windy, they worked inside, plastering cracked, dingy walls and sanding the pine plank floors.

Oso constructed a dirt-floored "office" in a disused hen-house, where he worked steadily on his dissertation, often late into the night. His typewriter, books, notebooks, and reams of paper cluttered his makeshift desk, a door balanced on sawhorses. Over the entrance, he hung a sign in crimson with white letters that read "The Harvard Coop."

Starshine set about making the plain adobe a homier place. She painted the kitchen yellow and their bedroom red with a deep blue ceiling she studded with reflective foil stars, planets, and moons. She made curtains out of her Indian print bedspreads. She hung her collection of concert posters, reserving the place of honor above the bed for her prized psychedelic Bob Dylan poster. She tossed incense onto the logs in the fireplace and burned scented candles in the windows.

Evenings found her sitting on a small, wooden chair in front of the fire, crafting lacey macramé necklaces and beading flowers, birds, and rainbows onto denim clothing she consigned to a Santa Fe gallery.

She missed her family in Wisconsin. Her parents were astonished and upset that she had abandoned her full-ride scholarship. But she wrote them lively, weekly letters recounting her life in the fabulous, exciting state of New Mexico with "friends," making no mention of her burly bed partner.

Oso often kept Starshine company while she futzed in the kitchen. He strummed his guitar, passed her joints, sang to her in his dark, mesmerizing voice as she made yoghurt, rinsed alfalfa sprouts, baked bread, and canned pickles, jam, and fruit. He marveled at her culinary competence.

"Blame Janet," Starshine said. "She passed on her Midwestern farm-wife skills to me. My mother can barely boil water."

Starshine easily settled into a pastoral life with Oso in Los Llanos. The disappointment of law school and the unnerving social and political turmoil of Berkeley became distant memories. "Every time I think of that place," she told Oso, "with that asshole Duck Dickworth on my case all the time, it gives me the shivers."

Starshine kept busy with her projects, but she was a little lonely in a town where locals were suspicious or down-right hostile to "los hippies." Her neighbor, Felicia Madrid, was one of the few who said hello to her when their paths crossed. Starshine decided maybe it was up to her to make the first friendly move. She bought a half-dozen speck-led bananas at the mom-and-pop mercantile eight miles away and set to baking banana bread. She appeared at the Madrids' door carrying a warm loaf wrapped in waxed paper, tied with a bit of red ribbon. "Hi, I'm your neighbor, Starshine."

"Oh, yes, I see you at the post office. Come on in," Mrs. Madrid said, holding open the screen door.

"I baked a loaf of banana bread for you. I hope it turned out OK. I followed the high-altitude adjustments in my *Joy of Cooking*."

"I love banana bread. How did you know? Once my hus-band, Arturo, sees it, it'll disappear fast. Do you have time for a cup of coffee?"

The conversation was a little awkward at first. Mrs. Madrid—"Please call me Felicia"—reminded Starshine of her grandmother, although she was closer in age to her mom. She was sunny, loved a good laugh, and made Starshine feel at home immediately. Arturo came in from the barn and spotted the loaf on the oilcloth-covered kitchen table. "Eeee, my favorite," he said and cut himself a generous slab.

Felicia knocked on Oso and Starshine's door a couple of days later and presented them with a plate of pumpkin-filled empanadas.

"Wowee!" Oso said, charging into the turnovers like a lion deprived for weeks of Christians.

Felicia nudged Starshine. "You'd better move fast or you won't get anything but crumbs."

The women became fast friends. With tutorials from Felicia, Starshine learned to cook on a wood stove, prune the homestead's apple trees, tend a small flock of goats, and make cheese from their milk. Felicia gave Starshine a couple of hens. "These girls are no spring chickens, but if you keep them warm and feed them table scraps, they'll lay eggs for you now and then. In April, you can get some chicks from the feed store. Be sure to ask for the ones that have been sexed. One look at you hippies, and they'll try to give you nothin' but roosters."

Oso offered to help Arturo with his projects. Together they fenced a pasture and put a new roof on the Madrid's barn. Arturo called Oso "Mr. Bear."

Arturo ran into Oso at the gas station on a balmy September day. "Hey, Mr. Bear, you want to go duck hunting next weekend? Around this time every year, my brothers, Joe and Leo, come up from Albuquerque, and we go after blue-wing teal in Colorado. Joe's got two black Labs. They're first-rate bird dogs."

"That sounds cool, Arturo. If my old lady says it's OK, I'd love to go with you. Teal are a real challenge, I hear. How long will we be gone?"

"A few days. My brothers and I have a tent, but you're a big fellow. You'll need to bring your own sleeping gear."

"I could drive Buster. It's got a bed in it as well as a hot plate and a fridge. We can camp out in luxury."

"Perfecto. Truth is, we need a second vehicle anyway. Can't fit four men, two dogs, and all our gear in one pickup."

Oso talked to Starshine.

"You'll have a swell time," she said. "Go."

"Can you manage OK without a car? Don't count on Janis Jalopy, Sweet Pea. I think she's had it."

"I don't need to go anywhere. Of course, I'll be all right. Besides, I've got tons of Christmas orders for beadwork to get out."

Starshine got her period two days after Oso left. It was never very regular; now it was early, and she had run out of Tampax. She called Felicia and explained the situation.

Felicia laughed. "I'm too old for all that business," she said. "Sorry, I can't help you out. I'd give you a ride to the merc, but I don't even know how to drive."

Starshine looked out the window at Janis. The LeSabre sat beneath an aged apple tree like a snoozing cat, the strong Western sun mellowing her once bright yellow paint job. She rarely used Janis except as a retreat, a place to sulk when she and Oso had a spat. Starshine hadn't driven the car in months, although she started her up now and then, and let her run for a while to keep the battery charged. The tires weren't flat, and the gas tank was half-full.

She went outside and addressed the car hopefully. "Janis, baby, you can make it to the merc, can't you?" she implored. "It's not that far. If you get me there, I'll give you some nice fresh gas. Put a little air in your tires. Wash your windshield. Please, please, please?"

Janis started right up. "Good girl," Starshine said happily and patted Janis on the dash.

Starshine left a note for Oso in case he came back early, and smoked a joint to ease her cramps. With the engine rattling badly, she drove fifteen miles an hour, pulling over to the side of the road whenever a faster car wanted to pass.

At the store, she bought two boxes of Tampax, adding essential supplies for a woman having a bad case of the monthly munchies—three Hershey bars, a bag of potato chips, a package of Little Debbie Cakes, a tin of cashews, and a fifth of bourbon.

The engine knocked rhythmically on the drive home, louder than ever, especially on the inclines. The entire body shook as if it had the DTs. "Come on, Janis," Starshine pleaded. "Try, try, try, just a little bit harder."

She drove even slower with her fingers crossed, praying the car would at least get her home. Topping the last rise, she cheered when the pitched tin roof of the house came into view and glided downhill in neutral. On the flat, she put the LeSabre back into gear. Ten yards before the drive-way, she signaled a left turn. She was halfway across the oncoming lane when a terrifying bang under the hood con-vulsed the car. Janis stopped dead in her tracks. Car parts clanged onto the roadbed; oil pooled beneath the engine; the interior filled with thick blue smoke. Coughing, chok-ing, and terrified, Starshine flung the door open and leaped out. "Shit, Janis. Are you on fire?"

With one hand on the steering wheel and the other on the frame, she tried to push the LeSabre the rest of the way across the road into the yard. "Jesus H. Christ, Janis. Your timing sucks!"

The car was unbelievably heavy and slow moving. Star-shine leaned further into her push, straining her whole body. Through the haze, she saw a propane truck rapidly bearing down on her. She froze. As the propane truck's brakes squealed shrilly, Starshine clenched her eyes shut and awaited the fiery crash. When she heard the truck door slam, she opened her eyes.

The driver came running toward her. "What the fuck are you doing, lady? Are you trying to kill us both?" he hollered.

"My engine just blew up. Help me get this goddamn tub off the road, will ya?"

Starshine and the gruff propane man were able to push the LeSabre into the yard. When it rolled to a stop beneath a cottonwood, he stood up and looked at it sadly. "Too bad about your ranfla, lady. She was a beauty."

Starshine nodded glumly. "Yeah, that old fart in Espa-ñola was right about her throwing a rod." She held out a five dollar bill to the man. "Thank you for your help. And for not crashing into my car."

"That's OK, lady," he said, refusing to take her money.

Starshine retrieved her grocery bag from the front seat. With Rez Dog at her heels, she wandered into the house in a daze.

Oso came home late that night to find her in the bathtub up to her chin in pink bubble bath, tipping back a half-empty bottle of Wild Turkey. Candy bar wrappers, a cellophane cupcake package, a potato chip bag, and an empty cashew tin littered the bathroom floor.

"Rough day, Sweet Pea?" he asked, scratching his beard.

"Whatever gives you that idea?" she slurred. She took another swig from the bottle and passed it to him.

Oso had bagged a dozen teal. Arturo and his brothers gave him another eight. He proudly carried a limp, bloody, still-feathered duck into the bathroom to show Starshine. "Purty, ain't he? I thought you could use the feathers in your beading. You'll have all twenty of them plucked in no time flat."

Starshine looked at the little duck and gagged. Its dead, vitreous eyes, its wet-feather smell, the gamey scent of Oso's blood-splattered overalls were too much for her. "Listen, O Great White Hunter," she grumbled. "You shot 'em; you clean 'em."

Oso laughed. "I already did, Sweet Pea. We breasted them out in camp, except for this one. I brought him for show and tell. I'm pullin' your chain."

———————————

It took Starshine a couple of days to recover from the worst hangover of her life and to be able to consider food again. Oso wrapped up half the duck breasts and froze them. He sliced the remaining ones into strips, sautéed them in butter with scallions, added a few juniper berries, a splash of white wine and served them over brown rice sprinkled with chopped parsley.

"This is delicious," Starshine said. "Forget filet mignon."

"They are indeed sweet and delectable. They were tricky to bring down. Fast little bastards. But they're more than worth the effort."

Over dessert, Starshine brought up the subject of a new car. "Oso, I need my own wheels, so I can run errands and deliver my things to galleries."

"Yup," he said. "The LeSabre's patas arriba. Your beloved Janis Jalopy is history, Sweet Pea. It'd be too expensive to put a new engine in her. She's New Mexico lawn sculpture now."

"Yeah, I suppose I can plant petunias in the trunk and let the hens nest in the back seat."

"Excellent idea." He smoothed his moustache and smiled at her slyly. "You know, you'd look real cute driving a pickup with your red hair flying out the window and Rez Dog in the back."

"That's either a New Mexico cliché or a sexist remark."

"Probably both, Sweet Pea," Oso laughed. "The truth is, Buster's no pickup. We sure could use one for dump runs and hauling things like goats, fence posts, and firewood. And you could use it to transport the enormous bags of money you're making with your beaded couture. Hey—and we could score lots of really fab road kill."

"Yum. I'll check the *Joy of Cooking* for road kill recipes."

"Say, you know Pito Mondragón?"

"The mechanic down the road who's some kind of preacher?"

"That's the one. He's got a '52 Chevy pickup parked out in front of his house with a $450 price tag on it. Can't say I think much of his attempt at a camouflage paint job or the Bondo on its left fender. If it runs well, do we care what it looks like?"

"No. But I only have $600 left to my name. Let's sleep on it."

"Excellent idea. Whaddaya say we climb into bed immediately and start gettin' relaxed?"

PART II La Troca

A descending half-moon and the light of a billion ancient stars helped two men find their way across an arroyo toward a small patch of drying corn rustling in the breeze. The stocky one held the leash of a pit bull that was straining forward, badly wanting to wander.

"Queenie ain't used to being on a leash," he whispered to his partner, a short, chubby man wrapped in an oversize plaid flannel jacket.

"Eeee, not long now, and we'll be partyin' big time, Pito."

"Shhhh, not so loud. We don't want the hippies' dog telling them we're here. That is one crazy, mean mother-fucker."

"The dog or Oso?"

"Both of 'em—locos."

No sooner had the words left Pito's mouth than a furious barking erupted from the far side of the cornfield. A huge black shape shot out of the stalks, streaking toward the men and their dog.

"Shhhhhit!" they said in unison. The short man struggled to pull a revolver from his pocket, but Pito put out a hand to stop him. "Put the gun away, Renzo. Here's why we brought Queenie. Watch this," he said with glee, unsnapping the dog's leash.

The pit bull zigzagged toward the male dog, which stopped barking, slowed his approach, and began scenting the air. Like a guided missile honing in on a target, he raced toward the female, wagging his tail energetically. He avidly sniffed her fore and aft. Though the smaller dog yelped and tried to squirm out of his reach, he easily overpowered her. Joined, the dogs whimpered, their tongues hanging out as they rocked back and forth.

"Praise the Lord! We're in business," Pito whispered excitedly, hurrying toward the corn patch.

The men waded into the field. Pulling burlap sacks and hedge clippers from their pockets, they attacked the woody stalks of tall green leafy marijuana plants scattered among the corn, hacking at them furiously.

From a few rows away, a deep voice interrupted them.

"You need the right tool for the job, hermanos. Them hedge clippers ain't gonna work. Mighty neighborly of you to help me bring in my crop, though."

A big, bearded man parted his way through the wavering plants, the moonlight faint but strong enough to illuminate his wide grin, the long sleeve shirt underneath his overall straps, and the gleaming twin barrels of the shotgun he cradled in his left arm.

"Now this here's what ya need," he said, swinging a wide-bladed machete with his right hand. Light from the heavens glinted off its razor-sharp edge as he lifted it above his head. A swooshing sound slashed the air, and several marijuana stalks clattered to the ground.

"Uh, we're out lookin' for our dog, Oso, and, uh, it looks like we found her," Pito stammered.

"Yeah," Renzo added, hastily shoving his clippers and bags into his pockets. "Looks like we found her. And so did your dog," he laughed nervously.

The bearded man nodded pensively, letting the machete drop to his side. "Rez Dog/pit bull puppies . . . scary. How 'bout a shot of Jim Beam, boys? It's a chilly night for September."

"Sure is," Renzo said enthusiastically.

Pito looked at the ground. "I, uh, I'm not a drinkin' man, Oso," he said. "It's not the Lord's way."

"No offense, Pito, but the Lord himself was a winemaker. We've got Boone's Farm Apple Wine if you'd rather."

"Well, just this once. Jim Beam will do."

Starshine woke up when Oso came back to bed, reeking of whiskey and the ever-present scent of cannabis. "Did you catch them?" she asked.

"Yup," he replied. "Put the fear of God into 'em."

"Who was it?"

"Reverend Pito and his cousin Renzo. Now maybe they'll leave my crop alone. And maybe a little guilt will soften up Pito on the truck price, too. Tomorrow might be an opportune moment to work out a deal with him. He'll be super hungover."

"I don't know," Starshine said. "Should we be doing business with Pito? When I went to borrow Felicia's apple peeler yesterday, I mentioned we were thinking of buying that pickup from him. 'You be careful,' she told me. 'Arturo always keeps his hand on his wallet when he has dealings with The Reverend, especially when he starts in on his Jesus talk.' In the morning, I'll tell you the story she told me about their experience with him last Thanksgiving."

"Can't wait," Oso said. He snuggled into her shoulder, kissed her on the cheek, and was out in seconds.

Starshine related Felicia's tale over breakfast.

"I always bake two turkeys at Thanksgiving for our family meal," Felicia had said, "so our guests can have leftovers to take home, 'cause everybody knows leftovers are the best part. Last spring, I decided to grow my own turkeys. Those birds, they're not all that smart. You have to raise them with hen chicks, or they won't know how to eat. I started out with six, and four of them made it. They got pretty big, especially because I was feeding them cracked corn as the holidays approached. The three toms weighed thirty pounds or more, the one hen maybe twenty-five. When Pito came by the house one day, he saw the turkeys in my pen. 'Them's mighty fine lookin' birds you got there,' he said. 'The wife's raisin' some, too. Maybe we should get together before Thanksgiving for a matanza at our place to slaughter the turkeys.'

"Well, it seemed like a good idea to us, because it's a lot of work, and neither one of us likes to chop their heads off after we've spent so many months taking care of them. So we said OK. On the way to the pen to catch the birds, Arturo went into the barn and came out with a can of blue paint.

" 'What do you want with that?' I asked him.

" 'You'll see,' he said. We tied their legs together, and he took a stick and made a little blue spot so small you could barely see it at the top of each turkey's legs. Then we put them in feed sacks in the back of the pickup and drove to Pito's.

"Pito chopped off the heads of their three and our four, and hung them to drain from the rusty jungle gym out by his barn. It looked a little creepy, with blood dripping onto the swings and the teeter-totter. I mean, Pito's grandkids still use that. Anyway, when the birds were well drained, we dipped each one in hot water and pulled off the feathers. Their turkeys were skin and bone. I don't think they fed them much. If they weighed out at twelve pounds, it was a lot. Anyway, after we finished plucking the birds, Arturo gutted them and set aside the giblets and necks. Pito's wife filled the kids' plastic swimming pool with ice water. It was one of those round things with duckies and puppies on it. Yuck! That's where we put the turkeys to cool down. It took the four of us the whole afternoon to finish the seven birds. We were dead tired by the time we were done and cleaned up the place.

"Pito came out with a wash bucket and slipped four cooled down turkeys into it. Then him and his wife headed toward their kitchen, each holding a side of the tub.

" 'Hold it,' Arturo said.

" 'Oops,' Pito said. 'Oh, yeah, you had four and we had three.' He put the smallest turkey back into the kiddie pool. Then they took off with the remaining three birds.

"Arturo stopped them again. 'Sorry, bro. You've got the wrong birds. Each one of ours has a little blue paint spot on its legs. Right, Felicia?'

" 'Yes, sir,' I said. Sure enough, they were carrying off our big, fat birds and leaving us their scrawny ones.

"We took our turkeys back, added the other blue-spotted one from the kiddie pool, put them in our big plastic tub and got out of there pretty quick. Once we were away from their place, we laughed ourselves sick!"

"Your husband's no dummy, is he?" Starshine said.

"He sure isn't. He may not have much schooling, but he can read people fast as lightning," she laughed. "Listen to me. When you have any dealings with The Reverend, keep your eyes wide open."

"Hmmm," Oso said. "Sounds like excellent advice. Pass the jam, wouldya, Sweet Pea?"

"So do you really think we need that very truck?"

"Yup, I do. For one thing, it's right up the road. If it breaks down, Pito can fix it."

Oso called The Reverend and made a time in late morning to look at the pickup. Optimistic they would be able to drive it home, they walked the half mile to Pito's house. The truck was parked outside the garage where Pito worked on cars and farm machinery. Inside, they found him bent over the engine of an ancient tractor, his jeans sliding down his wide, flat butt to reveal a dark crack that reminded Starshine of the Taos Gorge. His pit bull Queenie was asleep, chained to an engine block. When their voices woke her out of her nap, she began to bark furiously, her teeth bared as she lunged at the strangers, spittle flying. Pito looked up at Oso and Starshine, grinned, hiked up his jeans, and wiped his greasy hands on an even greasier rag.

"This here troca ain't handsome," he said. (An understatement, Starshine thought.) "But she's reliable, and the tires are fairly new. She'll get you where you need to go. And," he added enthusiastically, "unlike that Buick of yours, back home, too! Start 'er up. The engine runs good." He handed Oso a bundle of keys.

Oso cranked up the motor, which sputtered, caught, and let loose with several loud backfires that roused the barnyard into a cacophony of crowing, squawking, and barking protests. "Let's go out on the road for a spin," he said to Starshine.

"Oh, no," Pito said. "You can't take it outta the yard."

"Really? Why not?" Oso asked.

"Nope. Absolutely not. I don't have no insurance on

'er. I'm a law-abiding, God-fearing, Christian man. It'd be against the law for you to take 'er out on the highway. That's my rule."

"OK," Oso said reluctantly.

Pito did allow them to drive the truck around his bumpy yard for a few minutes. Grinning, he watched as they bounced from one gopher hole to another, dodging rocks, a snarling male pit bull trying to bite the tires, and several small barefoot children. They scattered a flock of chickens led by an outraged rooster that crowed angrily and attacked the truck with spread wings and slashing spurs.

Oso pulled to a stop next to Pito. He put on the parking brake and turned off the engine. "Well," he said slowly, "she seems to run pretty good. Will you take $400?"

"$450. Firm. And cash only. I'll bring 'er by after dinner tonight. I want to change out the spark plugs for you. Plus I gotta hunt up the title."

Oso and Starshine walked home, stopping every now and then for a hug and a smooch, pleased to have a new truck.

"I'd better get back to my beading," she said. "$450 is going to nearly wipe out my savings. But now with my own wheels, I can find more galleries I can sell to, like in Taos and Albuquerque. Whee!"

"Hey, Sweet Pea, before you get all tired out, how about a celebratory roll in the hay?"

Pito came by as promised with the pickup. Starshine paid him, and he signed over the title to her. The next morning, she and Oso decided to drive their new truck to Española to buy groceries. They weren't a hundred feet down the road when it became abundantly clear the truck had serious front-end problems. Even at five miles an hour, it wobbled dangerously and was practically impossible to steer.

Oso furiously spat out a string of expletives. He slammed on the brakes, jumped out of the truck, threw his gimme cap down on the ground, and stomped on it, simultaneously damning Pito and his entire lineage to an eternity of brimstone.

Starshine had never seen him so angry. His face was blood red. He punched the hood so hard his fist left a dent. She made him promise not to go after Pito. "Oso? Let's put the truck out by the highway with a sign on it and try to sell it," she said. "Caveat emptor, you know? It's our fault for trusting that son of a bitch."

"The fuck it is!" Oso yelled. "I'll get that goddamn sleazeball hypocritical bastard—you watch."

The pickup sat in their front yard with a For Sale sign on the windshield for a week before a pair of Mexican laborers in a battered, pea green Chevy Nova stopped to inquire about it.

"The engine is probably OK, but the front-end está chingado," Oso said. "Take it for a drive and see for yourselves."

The Mexicans were back in a few minutes. "You right," one said in broken English. "Know a mecánico who can fix it?"

Oso and Starshine looked at each other. "Everybody says the guy we bought it from is a decent garage mechanic,"

Oso said. "But he didn't tell us the alignment was fucked up. Now he says it'll cost $300 to fix the truck. We haven't got the money, so we're selling it for what we paid—$450."

"I be back later," the Mexican said.

The mexicanos drove down the road to Pito's. A quarter hour later, they returned. "We take the truck," one said. "You neighbor going to fix it. Then we come for it next month when we finish work up north." He took a wad of crumpled bills out of his pocket and paid Starshine.

"I'll get you the title," she said, disappearing into the house. Meanwhile, Oso and the Mexicans chatted away in Spanish, passing around a bottle of whiskey, joking, having a spontaneous party. Starshine laid the document down on the hood of the truck, signed it, and then watched one of the Mexicans scrawl an elaborate swirl of a signature on the paper.

Oso and the men emptied the whiskey bottle. Then Starshine saw him take something out of his overall pocket, hand it to one of the men, and slap him on the back. "¡Suerte, hermanos!" he laughed.

With one man driving the wobbly truck out of the yard, and the other following in the Nova, the Mexicans headed for Pito's house.

Felicia came by two weeks later to borrow Starshine's canning pressure cooker, Oso's birthday present to her in August. "I'm putting up stewing hens for the winter. It's so much faster with a pressure cooker," she said. "Mine broke last year. Maybe my Santa Claus will bring me a new one this Christmas."

"I'll find the opportune time to drop a little hint to Arturo," Oso offered.

"Buena idea, Mr. Bear. Say, did you hear about Pito's troca?" she asked with a giggle.

"Now what?" Starshine and Oso said in unison.

"Eeee, you're gonna love this. You know how those Mexicans were going to come back for the truck after Pito fixed the front-end?"

"Yeah, and I heard he was charging them six hundred bucks for the job—twice what he was gonna charge us," Oso said. "The cabrón."

"So did he fix it?" Starshine asked.

"Sure. He called them in Colorado and told them it was ready. They said they'd come by Saturday afternoon. Only they came in the middle of the night on Friday and drove off with it."

Felicia was laughing so hard she could barely talk. "Arturo went over there early Saturday morning to use Pito's compressor to pump up his tires. He got there at the very moment when Pito discovered the truck was gone. He told me he's never heard such words coming out of the mouth of a man of God. He thought Pito was going to have a heart attack."

"Did he send the cops after the Mexicans?" Starshine asked.

"Why bother? By then, they were across the border for sure. Now his truck's down in Mexico somewhere. And he'll never see it again. They must have had an extra key for it."

Starshine eyed Oso suspiciously. "Where could they possibly have gotten another key?"

"We have a saying in Spanish," Felicia said, "A cada cochino le llega su sábado."

"What's that mean?" Starshine asked.

Oso grinned, took off his work gloves, and laid them on the kitchen counter. "Means sooner or later, every pig will get slaughtered."

Starshine shook her head. "You're baaaaad, Oso."

"Yup," he nodded in agreement. "And damn proud of it."

2
Green Eyes

A young woman's voice called out from the kitchen: "Grandma? Where's the sugar bowl?"

"In the cupboard by the stove, sweetheart. On the bottom shelf," Rachel Guenther replied.

The fall light through the west windows washed like a wave of mellow gold over the olive and ochre damask sofa where she sat working on a needlepoint cover for her piano stool. She had begun the task after her husband gave her the heirloom Bechstein upright as a wedding gift. "No time like the present," she thought when she picked up the project sixty years later. Lost in memories, she barely noticed as Stephanie set the tray down on an end table and prepared a mug of sweet, milky tea.

As Stephanie handed her the cup, the weight of an earthshaking announcement escaped the young woman's chest in a dramatic outburst. "Grandma Rachel, I think I'm in love."

"Come sit by me, Stephanie," Mrs. Guenther said, patting the pillow next to her, raising a swarm of dust motes that glittered in the slant of autumnal light like tiny, iridescent insects caught in aqueous amber.

"What is all this? You're barely fifteen. Aren't you a little young to be in love?"

Stephanie settled into the sofa with her own tea—no sugar, no milk—and kissed the elderly woman's soft, powdery cheek. "Oh, but Grandma, didn't you tell me you got married at seventeen?" she teased.

"Yes, you've got me there." Affectionately she tugged at the ponytail that gathered the girl's curly, walnut brown hair at the nape of her neck. "Although looking back on it, I don't think it was such a sensible idea."

"Why not?"

"Becoming a wife at such a young age, I confined myself to a small, sheltered world I already knew and cut off my other options."

"Like what?"

"I never made it to normal school, so I never became a teacher like I planned. I longed to see the world beyond Cottonwood Grove that I'd read so much about: New York, Paris, Rome, Cairo. After I married, the closest I ever got to a big city was Las Vegas, New Mexico."

"This two-bit town was the big city?" Stephanie was incredulous.

"And it was even smaller then than it is now."

Stephanie rolled her eyes.

"In fact, I'd never even seen Santa Fe until after your Grandpa Fred came home from World War II."

"Why not?"

"Sweetie, we were poor. Our sole means of transportation was Fred's father's truck. We lived with my in-laws miles from town."

"That must have been so boring."

"Fortunately, my mother-in-law was kind to me. Your Great-grandmother Seferina had no daughters and only two sons. I think she was glad for my company."

"Which one is she in that old photograph on your mantelpiece?"

"She's the stern looking woman standing behind your Great-grandfather Wilhelm, with her hand on his shoulder."

"It looks like she's digging her claws into him."

Grandma Guenther laughed. "She was no fading flower, for sure. But she was a good-hearted, generous woman."

"Wasn't the ranch exciting? I mean, with handsome cowboys and Apache raids and all?"

"Sweetheart, I'm old, but I'm not that old. Besides, we didn't raise cows. We raised sheep. No one ever describes life on a sheep ranch as 'exciting.' It's a lot of hard, dirty, stinky work. And I was expected to do my part."

"Like what?"

"In lambing season, we helped the ewes when they had trouble birthing and bottle fed their lambs if they rejected them or didn't make it. We didn't have a washing machine yet, not even the wringer kind, so I helped Seferina wash clothes on a washboard. If the wind wasn't blowing too hard, we hung the laundry on a clothesline. We raised chickens. We tended a garden, but sometimes we lost the whole thing to rabbits, gophers, or hailstorms. We cooked three meals a day for a crew of a six men, cleaned house, did a lot of canning, and made almost all our own clothes."

"Wow. What did you do for fun?"

"Fun? We drove the truck to church once a week—if you call that fun."

"Didn't you ever go to dances or parties with Grandpa Fred?"

"Aside from weddings and funerals, there weren't many social occasions. Frankly, we were too exhausted from hard work to kick up our heels much. I hardly ever saw my husband outside mealtime and bedtime."

"Well, but were you happy?"

"Was I happy?" Grandma Guenther wondered. "Living on the ranch was a shock for me, I admit. I'd led a comparatively privileged life in Cottonwood Grove, though it was no more than a village. There was a church, two bars, a grade school, and my father's mercantile store. I grew up surrounded by extended family and friends my own age. I worked a bit in my father's store, measuring out pounds of sugar and yards of calico—definitely light duties. The ranch was different. Physically demanding and often lonely, too."

Grandma Guenther looked off into a distant world only she could see, beyond the yellowing sycamores sheltering her Victorian house from New Mexico's unremitting fall sunshine. She slowly sipped her tea.

"Now, who's this young man you're so starry-eyed over, Steph'?"

"Teddy González. He is sooo hot, Grandma. He's incredibly strong. He can toss a hay bale over his head with one arm, and he's the quarterback on the football team, and he's, like, totally a hunk. And he has the most amazing green eyes."

"Looks aren't everything, sweetheart. And they're usually the first to go."

"He's also one of the best students in the junior class. He makes everybody laugh, even the teachers. He's going to be an astronaut."

Grandma Guenther raised eyebrows a shade darker than her permed gray hair. "Isn't he Ed and Alice González's son? The ones who live near the old synagogue?"

"Uh, huh. His mom's real nice to me. Last week, she invited me to stop by for lemonade after she saw me at football practice. I love to watch Teddy play."

"Eduardo González's grandson?"

Stephanie nodded yes. "He's named for his grandpa Edward—you know, Eduardo in Spanish."

"His great-grandfather was Eduardo, too. Could you pour me more tea, please?"

Stephanie refilled their mugs, then sat back down. Grandma Guenther studied her granddaughter thoughtfully. "I think it's time I told you a story," she said.

"Awesome. I love it when you talk about the olden days, when everyone drove farm trucks and wagons, when there weren't any malls or cars or cellphones, and houses didn't even have electricity."

"This story goes way back to the 1920s, about five years before I was born. Seferina told it to me not long after I married her son.

"One night, when everyone had gone to bed, a boy rode up to their ranch house and banged on the door, yelling for Seferina. 'Mrs. Guenther! My dad says for you to come quick. It's my mom. She's having a baby and it won't come out.' The boy was from a family that raised sheep and goats five miles away."

"Was Seferina a nurse?" Stephanie asked.

"Not really. She was a partera, a midwife. It was a skill she learned from her mother and her mother's mother."

"Wasn't there a doctor around?"

"The nearest one was in Las Vegas. My father's grocery store had the only phone in town, and it was usually out of order. From the panic in the boy's voice, Seferina knew she didn't have time to fetch the doctor—if he would even come for a penniless mexicana. While she gathered up her mid-wifing things, her husband saddled her mare, and another horse for the boy, whose mount was too lathered to make the return trip."

"Didn't anybody have a car?"

"Just the priest, and he wouldn't have helped."

"No? Why not?"

"He was a terrible grump from what I remember of him. He always smelled of whiskey and cigars. Like a lot of priests, he was probably terrified of women and their . . . 'female problems.' Seferina knew better than to bother him.

"She and the boy set off at a fast trot, disappearing into the moonless night, with nothing more than starlight and the dim outlines of a rutted trail to guide them to the fami-ly's simple adobe house. Seferina found Josefa, the mother, lying on the kitchen table, writhing in blood-soaked sheets, surrounded by wide-eyed, terrified children, the little ones whimpering and clutching at the older ones. Their mother was white as a frog's belly, bathed in sweat, and barely breathing after being in labor for twenty hours. The baby was early—way early—and a breech birth.

"Seferina yelled at the husband in Spanish as she went about tending to the woman. 'Why in hell didn't you send for me when she went into labor?'

"The man hung his head. 'I didn't send for you sooner because we don't have any way to pay you.'

"'That makes no difference to me,' Seferina grumbled. 'I'm not in this for money or chickens or anything else. All I care about is helping women have healthy children.'

"'Please save my wife. I don't know what I'll do if she dies on me.'

"'Fetch me some hot water and clean cloths. Then get out of here. And take these kids with you. They're scared to death.'

"Seferina finally managed to turn the baby around. It slipped out of its mother in a rush of bloody liquid. At first, she thought it was dead. It was no bigger than a newborn puppy, its large bulging eyes sealed shut, its tiny body a lump of pale wrinkles and pitifully thin appendages as it lay curled and motionless on the table between its mother's legs. She picked up the baby boy and patted him gently on his back. He was breathing, however faintly. She cut the umbilical cord, cleaned him up, swaddled him in strips of flannel, and placed him in a basket near the woodstove. Then she tended to the mother, massaging her belly to help expel the placenta.

"Josefa muttered in a weak, plaintive voice, 'My baby?'

"'He's alive,' Seferina told her. 'But he's awfully small, and I'm not sure he'll survive.'

41

"The mother's pale cheeks were wet with tears. With what little strength she had, she sobbed until sleep overcame her.

"Seferina gathered up the tiny swaddled infant and went out into the hall, closing the kitchen door behind her. She showed the baby to his father, who regarded him as he would a piece of torn strap leather or a busted tool.

"'A boy, huh? Got no use for another one,' he mumbled. 'Is he gonna make it?'

"Seferina shrugged. 'I don't think so. He can't weigh more than a pound and a half. He's very early. His lungs aren't well enough developed at this stage.'

"'Maybe you should take him.'

"'Me? What would I do with him? Assuming he survives—and I doubt he will.'

"'If he lives, maybe a family around here could use an extra boy. I've already got six of 'em, plus the two girls. We're barely getting by as it is. Besides, I don't think Josefa can manage with a sickly infant.'

"Seferina shook her head in dismay. 'I told you when I delivered the last one that she shouldn't have any more kids for at least a couple of years. She's exhausted and probably anemic. What were you thinking? You've already got eight kids, and the last one's not a year yet."

"'I know, I know. But Padre Domínguez says we should accept as many children as God sends us,' the man whined, wiping his mournful, red-rimmed eyes with the back of his dry, calloused hand.

"'I'll ask Josefa when she wakes up what she'd like to do. She ought to have some say in the matter.' "

Stephanie interrupted her grandmother. "You mean the parents were going to give their baby away, just like that?"

"Sweetheart, people did that all the time. Those who already had too many kids gave infants away to families that had none or had lost children. Or a couple too young to be parents gave their firstborn to the grandparents to raise, to keep them company as they got up in years. Here in New Mexico, grandparents still raise kids their own children can't take care of for one reason or another."

"I think it's awful when people give away their babies. Three girls in my class have already gotten pregnant this year. But they're going to keep them."

"Steph', sweetheart, giving away a baby you can't care for is often the best thing. The child might have a better chance with people who want him and can provide for him. Teen pregnancies are really stupid. Girls should use their brains, keep their legs together, and not go off with boys like their pants are on fire. I don't care how 'hot' their boyfriends are."

"Grandma!"

"Am I shocking you?"

"Uh, yes."

"Look, you can have babies until you're at least forty-five. So why have one before you've finished school, before you can support one, before your boyfriend is a man? Why don't these kids use birth control?"

"Didn't they use birth control in those days?"

"No. There weren't any pills or diaphragms or condoms. There were no abortions—although if the truth be told, the curanderas often used herbs to help women terminate unwanted pregnancies. Women always know when it's a good time to have a child and when it isn't."

Stephanie's eyes went wide.

"I know you're wild about this boy, Steph', but you're way too young for sex."

The girl looked down at her hands grasping the tea mug and grinned shyly.

"I'm dead serious, young lady. Sleeping with a boy at your age is a dumb, reckless thing to do."

Stephanie knew her face was flushed. She looked away.

"Let me guess. Your mother never talked with you about sex."

"Not really. She left a copy of *The Joy of Sex* lying around, and I suppose us kids were supposed to figure it out for ourselves."

Grandma Guenther sighed. "I love my daughter-in-law, but really, she ought to know better. She's a psychologist."

Stephanie decided it was time to change the subject. "So Grandma, what happened to that baby?"

"Ah, yes, the baby. It was clear neither of his parents much wanted him, nor could Josefa care for a weak infant, so Mother Guenther put him in her apron pocket and brought him home."

"She put him in her *pocket*?"

"Yes. She always wore a midwife's apron when she delivered a baby. It had big pockets in front. He'd be warmer there next to her body, under her coat while she rode home."

"What did her husband say when she showed up with him?"

"Knowing your Great-grandfather Wilhelm, not a lot, I'd guess. He rarely went up against her. Besides, nobody believed the baby would live. She probably thought she was doing his family a favor. When he died, it would happen out of their sight, and it wouldn't be so traumatic for them. Maybe she wanted another child. In those days, they had one son, your Great-uncle Harold, and he was preparing to leave the ranch for high school in Las Vegas."

"Did the baby make it?" Stephanie asked in a tiny, hopeful voice.

"Against all odds, he did. Seferina carried him everywhere in her pocket, like a kangaroo, and fed him evaporated milk formula. He had a healthy appetite, and gradually, he grew stronger. When he was less than two weeks old, he nearly died though. He was saved by the family cat."

"Wow. Tell me *that* story."

"Shortly after Seferina brought the baby home, your Great-grandfather returned late one cold, blustery night from a grange meeting. As usual, he came in through the kitchen. The house was dark, Seferina was asleep, and he didn't want to light a lamp. As he made his way toward the bedroom, he ran smack into the open door of the oven, banging his shin. He cursed his wife for leaving it ajar and slammed it shut. He undressed in the dark and got into bed. He was nearly asleep, when their cat began to yowl from the kitchen, so persistently that it woke up Seferina.

"'What is the matter with Seisi? She never meows like that.'

"'That goddamn six-toed weirdo,' Great-grandpa Guenther groused. 'I should have drowned her the same time I drowned her kittens. She's probably in heat again.'

"The cat continued to howl. Seferina threw back the bedcovers. 'Something is wrong. I'm going to investigate.' She got out of bed and followed the yowls to the kitchen.

"'Oh, my God, the baby!' she shrieked.

"Her husband tore out of bed and ran into the kitchen where he hastily lit a kerosene lamp. Seferina was standing by the oven, clutching the tiny newborn in her arms, swaying with him and kissing him.

"The night was unusually cold, and the house was drafty, so Seferina had placed the swaddled infant in a roasting pan and put him in the oven so the pilot light would keep him warm. She carefully left the door open, so he'd have enough oxygen and wouldn't get overheated. Great-grandpa nearly killed him when he closed the oven door."

Stephanie listened with wonder. "Was the baby OK?"

"He was unharmed. If it wasn't for Seisi, though, he might not have been. After that, the cat hovered over him, following Seferina wherever she took him. It was like she didn't trust the humans to take care of him. She liked to curl up with the baby in his basket, lick his face and smooth his hair with her tongue as if he was her kitten."

"Was that Seisi the great-grandmother of the Seisi you have now?"

"Probably the great-great-great-great-great-grandmother of ours. We've always had those calicoes, and they've always been called Seisi, for their six toes—seis in Spanish.

46

Seferina told me the first ones came from Germany when the Guenther family emigrated."

"And the baby, Grandma? Did he live very long?" She asked with trepidation.

Rachel smiled. "Let's see. I'm seventy-nine, and your Grandpa Fred is five years older than me, so he must be eighty-four now."

"Oh, my God. Grandpa Fred was that baby? He's so big and strong. He still chops firewood and drives a truck. A stick shift!"

"He is indeed that baby. He may have shrunk a little by now, but he grew up to be at least six feet tall."

"Does he know he was adopted?"

"Of course. Everyone in Las Vegas knows he was born into the González family. It never has mattered. Until now, that is."

"So why does it matter now, Grandma?"

She smiled, put her arm around her grandchild's shoulders, and kissed the top of her head. "Because your Grandpa Fred is also your darling Teddy González's Great-uncle Fred, sweetheart. His grandfather and your grandfather are brothers. Which means you and Teddy are cousins."

Stephanie thought for a while. "So what's the big deal? I mean, if Teddy and I had kids—like when we were much, much older," she grinned, "would it be a problem?"

"You know, sweetheart, cousins who marry run a higher risk of having kids with inherited diseases and birth defects. They might well have those startling green eyes like Teddy and my Fred and many of the Gonzálezes, but they might also turn out cross-eyed or have six toes like Seisi. Don't they teach you kids about DNA in biology class?"

"We haven't gotten there yet. Maybe next semester."

"It's high time you learned the basics. Let's go crank up the computer your father gave me. I don't even know how to turn the damn thing on yet, but I hear you can tootle oceans of information."

"Grandma—it's 'Google,' not 'tootle.' Surfing the net is a piece of cake. Let me show you how."

Rachel Guenther smiled. "I'd love that. Let's see if you can drag this doddering fossil into the twenty-first century."

"Awesome, Grandma!"

3
carnales

The villagers of Ojo Claro, New Mexico, would long recall with a mix of outrage and bemused gusto that Procopio "Porky" Lucero was the first sheriff's deputy to respond to the standoff at the cemetery that steamy Memorial Day afternoon. His wife was one of their own, but Porky, who was from Española, was an outsider. Who knew where his loyalties lay?

Porky got the dispatcher's call while he was parked in the San Anselmo Casino parking lot peeling back the paper on a microwaved carne adovada burrito, his third of the day. He knew exactly where the Ojo Claro Cemetery was; his wife's ancestors were buried there. Setting the gumball machine twirling on top of his Crown Victoria, he zoomed down I-25 with his siren screaming and took the Ojo Claro exit. At a curve in the old highway that paralleled the interstate, he veered onto a dirt road that was more pothole than surface. The sedan bounded and swerved down the road like a drunken jackrabbit, skidding to a stop in front of the cemetery's high rock wall. There, a big-gutted, florid-faced man wearing a black suit and a wide red tie stood pointing a gleaming 30.06 at the couple dozen mostly old people inside the graveyard. A heavy chain was looped through the bars of the tall, wrought-iron gate, and an oversized padlock secured it.

Porky leaned out the open window of his Crown Vic, draping his meaty hand over the side mirror. "¿Qué pasa, Joe?"

"These people are trespassing on my land!" the man yelled, gesturing with the barrel of his rifle at his captives, many of them barely tall enough to see over the stone wall that imprisoned them.

Their faces as stony and chiseled as the headstones, the elderly cleanup crew had stopped chopping weeds to lean on their shovels and hoes and glare daggers at the man holding them hostage. Their dark, congealed, communal anger contrasted sharply with the sunny holiday and the cheerful decorations on the mounds of their ancestors' graves. Multicolored silk and plastic flowers, some bright and new, some tattered and faded, adorned nearly every plot. Here and there, small, perky American flags fluttered in a light breeze.

"Put the gun down, Joe," Porky said wearily, pulling on his parking brake and turning off the motor. He unfolded himself from behind the steering wheel and got out of the car, tugging his belt up over his paunch.

A siren's mounting crescendo announced the approach of another officer. Porky bent back into his car, retrieved his patrolman's cap, and jerked it down over his thick black hair. It could be his boss, Sheriff MacDermott. Porky tucked in his gut in an attempt to look taller, hoisted his pants up again, and asserted his authority. "Joe," he said, holding a hand toward the rifle as the sheriff drove up. "Gimme the gun. You know the cemetery's church property. This place has been a camposanto for two, three hundred years."

The man in the black suit narrowed his eyes. Noting the arrival of an authority higher than the pudgy deputy in his face, he clenched his jaw, tightened his grip on the gunstock, and snarled like a petulant brat refusing to give up his cap gun. "Fuck you, Porky."

The sheriff's car slid to a halt in a fog of dun colored dirt that engulfed everyone on both sides of the wall, setting off a collective coughing fit. A lanky, angular Anglo appeared like an apparition out of the dust cloud. Approaching the tense situation between Porky and a man holding a firearm, he calmly whacked his Stetson against his pressed tan uniform in an effort to rid it of dust, and unhappily noticed his once shiny, walnut brown cowboy boots were now powdered with the parking lot's rain starved soil. "What's going on here, Lucero?" he asked.

Porky tipped his cap to his superior in a perfunctory greeting. "This here's Joe Ortega, Sheriff MacDermott. He says these people are trespassing on his property."

Ortega casually tucked his rifle under his arm. Cloaking his face in a wide, toothy smile, he held out his hand like the backslapping veteran politician he was. "Joe Ortega, Sheriff MacDermott," he said, eagerly grasping the officer's hand. "Sure appreciate you men helping out here today to bring this situation under control."

Porky sighed to himself, shuffled his feet, and focused his gaze on the brilliant blue sky beyond the tops of the valley's leafy cottonwoods. If the call had come in fifteen minutes later, he would already be off duty, on his way home, ready to sack out in his La-Z-Boy and sip a cool one in front of the tube.

Ortega clutched the sheriff by the elbow and steered him off for a private conversation. They leaned against Ortega's lustrous emerald Cadillac, talking quietly, their eyes switching back and forth from the bare ground in front of them to briefly alight on the restless herd of sullen villagers glaring at them from inside their graveyard corral.

Then, as if a verbal dust devil were swirling through the cemetery, the congregation's mutterings gathered force, rising higher in pitch, becoming angrier and louder until their voices erupted in a chorus of catcalls. "Let us out of here, sheriff!" a tall, middle-aged man in a khaki jumpsuit hollered.

An irate, heavy-set woman, her entire body quivering as she shook her upraised fist, protested from behind the grille. "Ortega's got no right to keep us locked up!"

"Do the job we elected you to do, MacDermott!" another prisoner yelled.

"Yeah, sheriff, whose side are you on anyway?" sneered an ungainly teenager, thrusting his skinny chest forward with bantam bravado.

A dozen yards away, the sheriff and Joe Ortega scarcely lifted their heads at the commotion. They resumed their conference, turning their backs to the crowd. Each planted a boot on the bumper of Ortega's Cadillac; each dangled a limp arm from the beam of his cocked leg.

The captives continued to pelt Ortega and the sheriff with jeers and protests. Suddenly, the wail of a siren and a cloud of earthen smoke rolling down the road toward them announced the arrival of yet another patrol car.

Porky noisily inhaled through his crooked nose and adjusted his cap as the cop car skidded to a stop in a shower of dirt and gravel inches from his knees. A small, nut-brown man wearing a uniform two sizes too big popped out of the car, unholstered an oversized pistol, and pointed it at the detainees. Eyeing the young officer's weapon, the crowd suddenly fell silent and shrank back from the gate.

"Put the cuete away, Ramírez," Porky commanded, scratching a stubbly spot on his chin he had missed shaving that morning. "You ain't on TV. And this ain't no episode of *NYPD Blue*."

Trying to look as nonchalant as possible, Ramírez relaxed his two-fisted grip on the pistol, dropped his draw, and reholstered his gun. "So what the fuck's going on?" he whispered, his eyes studying the jittery, smoldering throng gathered behind the locked gate. "Shit, it's just a bunch of old people. What gives?"

"Politics," Porky groused. He jutted his chin toward the sheriff and Ortega, still in their huddle by Ortega's shiny green Caddy. "What you're witnessing is the power of money."

Ramírez looked confused. Porky shoved his hands into his pockets and explained. "That guy there is Joe Ortega. He owns most of the property around here, so he and his family are used to having everything done their way.

People say the Ortegas got rich after Joe's grandfather stole the ejido lands—the communal village lands—but they've never been able to prove it. Ortega has made a mint from mining the gravel on that land. What he's got his dick in a wringer about is a little dispute with the villagers. When he put up some monster billboards on I-25, half a dozen people in Ojo Claro sued him to get them taken down. And they won."

"This is about *billboards*?" Ramírez asked a little too loudly.

"Shhhh, pendejo," Porky hissed. "Yeah. You know, those monster signs with glitter and huge spotlights on them. Local folks hate them things. The ones advertising Indian casinos remind them that's where their hard-earned savings went, and the ones advertising fancy hotels in Santa Fe don't let them forget they'll never set foot in one of those places unless it's to fix a clogged toilet or make a bed. Then there's the billboard the state rents to brag about what a beneficial thing welfare reform is. Plus the lights shine in their windows at night."

"I'd be angry, too. Them things are lit up like a Juárez whorehouse," Ramírez said.

Porky continued. "I guess they don't comply with county zoning laws. Ortega is plenty pissed because his billboards have to come down. So when people came today to clean up the graves for Memorial Day, he padlocked them inside. Says they trespassed on his land. He doesn't own the camposanto—it's church property. But he claims the cemetery road belongs to him. He used his cellphone to call his brother-in-law, the state senator, while he held a gun on the people. Then the senator called us."

"What a bunch of crap," Ramírez said. "Where are we, Mars? It's illegal to hold people hostage like this."

"You newcomers," Porky muttered. "This is Nuevo México. This is how things work here. I bet it wasn't no different in your country."

Ramírez bristled and stretched upward to his full height of five feet five. "Hey, I'm an American. My parents are Puerto Rican, but I'm from Jersey, and I'm just as American as you are. I've never even been to PR."

"Well, I bet things in Jersey or Puerto Rico or wherever ain't no different," Porky said, rubbing his thumb and fingers together in the universal sign for money. "Anyways, we're roasting our brains out in the hot sun doing that rich SOB's dirty work, and if you ask me, it sucks. Some of them people are ancient. The cabrón—he's got no right to keep them in there."

"How do you know such a lot about who's who, Lucero? I thought you were from Española."

"I am, but I've worked this area a long time. My wife's family, the Chacóns, founded Ojo Claro. Her mom still lives here, and this is where her dad's buried. Plus Ortega and my dad are related."

"Jesus, you're all primos in this place."

"Yup. One way or another, we're all cousins."

Suddenly the tall man in the khaki jumpsuit scrambled over the wall and strode calmly toward the sheriff. Ortega swung the rifle out from under his arm and aimed it at the man. The sheriff pushed the barrel down, keeping a firm grip on it.

"Uh, oh," Porky whispered to Ramírez. "It's Frank Mares, one of the guys who sued Ortega because of the billboards. His daughter's the abogada who won the case."

Mares called out to Ortega. "I gotta go home and get my heart pills, Joe. You don't want to be responsible for me having a heart attack, now do you?"

Ortega responded with a granite silence. The tanned leather of his face creased in an angry scowl. He narrowed his eyes at Mares and refused to take the hand offered him. Mares shrugged and shook hands with the sheriff. The three spoke quietly for several minutes, their arms folded, their boots toeing the gravel. Thirty feet away, the deputies leaned against Ramírez's patrol car, feigning disinterest while watching the conference intently out of the corners of their eyes like cats monitoring a birdbath. At one point, Ortega reddened and wagged his fist in Mares' face, yelling something unintelligible. Mares didn't back up or even blink. The sheriff put his hand on Ortega's shoulder, and the man dropped his arms to his sides, the downward pointing rifle paired to his left leg like an orthopedic brace.

After several more minutes of negotiations, Sheriff Mac-Dermott motioned to Porky. He snapped to attention, hiked up his pants, adjusted his cap, and joined the confab.

"Lucero, take Mr. Mares here to his house to get his heart pills," the sheriff said. "Then go by the church. He wants to talk to Father Ed. Says the priest might be able to help work this out."

Porky and Frank Mares got into Porky's patrol car and

barreled down Joe Ortega's road toward the center of town. As soon as the standoff faded into their dust-clouded side mirrors, the men leaned back in their seats and exhaled pent-up breath that escaped their lungs like air from a leaky balloon. Their eyes met, and they shared a nervous laugh.

"Sorry about this, Frank," Porky said.

"No problem, carnal," Mares said.

"Is it true you need heart pills? Shit, wasn't it last week you were a star pitcher, throwing curve balls for your high school baseball team in 'Burque? How'd you get so old so fast?"

Frank laughed. "Beats me, bro. Old age sneaks up on you like a tax collector. I had a heart attack last fall. The doc tells me to take it easy, quit frying my beans in lard, avoid stress. Ortega's bad for my health," he sighed.

"He's bad for everybody's health," Porky mumbled.

Frank pointed out a house across from the fire station. "Drop me off here. You can park under the cottonwood where it's shady. I'll be back in a flash."

Frank kept his word. Minutes later, he returned to Porky's squad car, a vial of pills rattling in the pocket of his overalls. They drove to the San Ysidro Parish, where they found the priest on his knees in the garden behind the rectory, weeding his rose bed. Mares described the confrontation to Father Ed. The white-haired priest frowned. He stood up slowly, brushed the dirt from the knees of his work pants, took off his garden gloves, and dabbed at his sweaty brow with a handkerchief.

"Do the people have water?" Father Ed asked. "It's a hot day, and there's not much shade there."

"Most of them were planning on working all day, so they brought water, food, and folding chairs with them," Mares said.

"Let's go then," the priest said.

Back at the cemetery, Porky stood off to one side as the priest, Mares, Ortega, and Sheriff MacDermott conferred. Their conversation was too low for Porky to hear, but he could see Ortega was still agitated. After nearly a quarter hour, Ortega spat on the ground. He drew a key out of his pocket and dropped it into the priest's extended hand.

Father Ed walked to the entrance with Frank Mares at his side. He undid the padlock and opened the gates. As the villagers spilled out into the parking lot, a number of them gripped the padre's hand and patted Frank Mares on the back. Then, trundling their tools, coolers, and chairs, they dispersed to their vehicles, looking back over their shoulders to glower at Joe Ortega.

One of the last people to leave the enclosure was a tiny, elderly woman with a red kerchief tied around her wispy white hair. Limping badly and leaning her weight on a single crutch, she approached Joe Ortega.

"Tía Lourdes!" he gasped. "I didn't know you were in there. What are you doing here?"

"¿Qué crees? I am cleaning up your grandparents' graves, malcriado," she said, her obsidian eyes fiery with molten anger. "Something none of you worthless Ortegas have ever done since your mother died—qué en paz descanse."

Ortega stiffened but said nothing.

The old woman jabbed his chest with a gnarled finger.

"You have no business locking people in or out of the holy ground, José. It's a gran pecado, hijo, a serious sin indeed. You disgrace your grandparents' memory and the memory of your mother and your father and all your ancestors. This is ejido land," she said, her thin, brown arm sweeping across the undulating expanse of rabbit brush and sand sage surrounding the burial ground. "It belongs to everyone. It's not yours and you know it."

Having said her piece, she hobbled off toward a battered pickup, where a young man lifted her bodily onto the front seat and drove away with her.

Frank Mares walked into a bar down the road from Ojo Claro several weeks later. Porky and Ramírez were having a beer after work. Porky waved Mares over. "Let me buy you a cold one, carnal," he said. "I owe you for that business at the camposanto."

Mares shrugged. "You don't owe me," he said. "You were just doing your job. We all know that. Besides, it got worked out."

The bartender placed a glass of beer down the bar in front of Mares. "It's on the house, Frank," he said.

"I gotta know," Ramírez said. "How'd you get Ortega to let the people out of there?"

"It took some talking," Mares said, taking a long draught of his beer.

"First Ortega told Father Ed he'd let everybody out except for six people—me and the other five who sued him because of the billboards.

"'We can't agree to that,' the padre said.

"Ortega got so red in the face, I thought he was going to explode. Then after a bit he said, 'OK, I'll let 'em go, and they can use my road, except for those six people.'

"The priest shook his head sadly. 'No deal, Joe.'

"'Well, actually, I've been thinking about giving the road to the Archdiocese,' Ortega said, drawing circles in the dust with the muzzle of his gun. 'But first, I want the Church to promise me something.'

"'Like what?' Father Ed asked.

"'I need an agreement that none of those six people can ever be buried in that cemetery.'

"The priest seemed really disgusted with Ortega. 'The Church will never go for that, Joe,' he said.

"Ortega stared at the ground for several minutes. Then he threw up his hands. The barrel of his gun was pointing at a huge thunderhead above them, like he maybe was gonna blow it out of the sky. 'OK,' he said angrily. 'I'll give the damn road to the Church anyway, but I want a tax deduction.'"

"That's a good one,' Porky said, slapping his hand down on the bar. "He wants a fucking tax deduction."

The men howled with laughter.

"That's not the end of it, though," Mares said. "I'll let you in on a little something else, but you have to swear you'll keep quiet about it."

The two deputies sat up straighter. "You got it, carnal," Porky said.

"Somebody walked into my daughter Monica's law office in Albuquerque a few days after the standoff and handed her an old document in Spanish. She showed it to a professor at the law school who can read those things. He thinks it's genuine, and it proves the villagers are correct about the ejido lands being theirs."

"Eeee," Porky said, grinning broadly. "So who was it? Who gave you guys that documento?"

Mares tipped the last of his beer down his throat and smiled. "Can't say," he said, sliding off the barstool and patting Porky on the shoulder. "Ay te watcho. Be seeing you."

Ramírez turned to Porky after he left the bar. "So, bro, you gonna break the news to Ortega? I bet he'd be very, very grateful if you told him about that document."

Porky regarded Ramírez with disdain. "I ain't saying nothin' to that cabrón. And you ain't neither, understand?"

"Gotcha, Porky. My lips are sealed."

"We're related, you know," Porky said.

"You mean you and Ortega?"

"Forget that, vato," Porky said. "I mean me and Mares. He's family. His mother's a Lucero; she's married to my dad's tío. And we Luceros stick together, hombre. We're carnales."

Ramírez nodded and took a final sip of his beer.

A slow grin slid across Porky's smooth, flabby jowl. "Let me buy you another one, dude. I'm celebrating."

His grin grew so wide that even in the bar's smoky, miserly light Ramírez could see the gleam from the gold cap on one of his molars.

"Celebrating? What's to celebrate?" Ramírez asked.

"If the villagers can prove the ejido lands are theirs, my wife could be a part owner of Joe Ortega's gravel mine," Porky said triumphantly. "I think that calls for another beer, don't you?"

"For sure, bro. As long as you're buying."

4

᠐UTT

To this day, I can't believe I actually paid money for Mutt—
ten bucks, I think.

I lived by myself in a sweet, little frame house in the
North Valley of Albuquerque in the late '70s, an area still so
rural that it was crisscrossed by irrigation ditches water-
ing small orchards and minifields of vegetables. Some
neighbors kept horses, goats, maybe a cow or two. It was
an idyllic spot, green and leafy. But unfortunately, a few
of my teenage neighbors were violent criminals. I freaked
out when Snake, the baddest of the bad, kidnapped a clerk
from a Circle K and dragged her onto the ditch bank a half-
block from my house. As he was preparing to rape her,
she grabbed his .22 and pistol-whipped him. Wahoo! Ten
points for our side! He was going to jail for a month or two,
but he had cousins in the neighborhood, so I thought I'd
better get some backup.

A dog was the answer. I decided I should start with a
puppy, so he would be loyal to me, trustworthy, and pro-
tective. How dopey can a girl be? Obviously, I had never
had a puppy. My neatnik German mother never allowed us
to have pets of any kind, not even a goldfish.

I looked in the paper for a likely prospect. A family in the Northeast Heights had eight-week-old puppies. Their ad claimed the pups were purebred German shepherds, so I called. "We just haven't bothered to get the papers," the man said, adding cheerfully, "Parents on premises."

I drove to the Heights with visions of Rin Tin Tin in mind—a brave, handsome, stalwart, full grown dog posed dramatically on a rocky outcropping, ready to defend a damsel in distress, specifically one in a precinct rife with young thugs.

I wasn't terribly surprised to find the only "parent" in sight was the man I had talked to on the phone, and the puppies didn't look anything like him. They were cute; he was sort of creepy. A beer belly threatened to pop the buttons of his none-too-clean shirt. His eyes were hooded, his wide face drooped, his down-turned mouth showed sharp teeth in a serious underbite. He looked more like an English bulldog than a German shepherd.

The puppies in the litter of seven were obviously mixed breed. Still, they were roly-poly, friendly, and who can resist puppies? They tumbled around in a dresser drawer lined with towels, chewing on each other's ears, tails, and snouts. I picked them up, one by one. They licked my hands, snuggling into my arms. Except a long-nosed, reddish one, who crept into a corner away from me and curled into a tight ball. I thought he showed good sense, so I chose him.

A fierce fanged, foaming at the mouth, monster dog was what I needed to protect me from the local marauders; a shy, fuzzy German shepherd cross puppy was what I got.

What a mistake. Mutt whined constantly. I tried to give him back. I was even willing to forego the $10, but Mr. Bulldawg said, "Nope. We got a no returns policy."

The dog continued his whimpering for weeks, keeping me awake all night. My ex-boyfriend/pal Art said putting a wind up alarm clock in the pup's milk crate might help calm him down. Its rhythmic ticking and tocking would remind him of his mother's heartbeat. I bought a cheap model at Woolworth's to put in his box, but Mutt kept up his noisy, nocturnal lament. One morning, I caught him trying to shove the clock under the stove with his nose. Maybe its clatter annoyed him as much as it did me.

I was almost ready to tie Mutt in a sack of rocks and drop him into the irrigation ditch when he began to sleep through the night. Not a moment too soon.

Even more vexing than the crying was Mutt's penchant for peeing everywhere in my little frame house except on my prized hand-woven Mexican rugs, where he laid large, messy plops of poop. Again, I regretted my starter-dog purchase, but being a softie, I couldn't abandon him to the puppy killers at the pound.

Instead, I went to the library, where I checked out a book about how to raise a dog. I tried the newspaper thing, hoping to get him to do his duty on the paper in my linoleum floored entryway. He ignored my plan and continued to use my entire house as a toilet. I kept working on it. I would stick his nose in the puddle, swat him on the rump with a newspaper, and take him outside. Eventually, he got the idea, but chose my grouchy, next-door neighbor Mrs. Kubler's lawn as his designated dumping spot. In spite of my best efforts to follow him with a plastic sack and a scooper whenever he headed for her yard, the grass was soon dappled with brown spots, the annals of his intestinal productions. Mutt also loved peeing on the tires of her prized cream and Pink Panther pink 1960 Dodge Dart Pioneer parked in her driveway. Gradually, her whitewalls became yellow walls. I wasn't always fast enough for Mutt or for Mrs. Kubler. She would call Animal Control on me.

Next Mutt went into his chewing phase. He didn't go after my beat-up tennis shoes or Kmart flip-flops. No, he chose my wedding and funeral high heels, a pair of lovely, red, Italian leather pumps I bought on sale in D.C. and reserved for special occasions. I didn't notice the shoes were missing until suspicious shreds of red leather showed up in his doo on Mrs. Kubler's lawn.

I got him knucklebones at the supermarket in hopes of curing him of his chewing habit. He didn't much care for them. Instead, he set about eating the homemade Taos bed I used as a sofa. I went to the Goodwill, where I bought a pair of beat-up, red Ferragamos, size ten, which I left by his water dish in the kitchen. Mutt ignored them until it occurred to me that perhaps an important part of his shoe fetish might be thieving footwear from my closet. I put them in with my flip-flops. A few days later, I found red shoe parts all around the house, the yard, and next door in his output.

Mutt liked to be outside; he joyfully took off at every opportunity. If I opened the door a crack to go out to my mailbox, he blasted through me like I was tissue paper, blithely trotting down the street or the ditch bank. I tried to teach him to come, holding out treats to tempt him. But he was wily. He'd ignore me, or he'd dance out of my reach so I couldn't grab him. With a toss of his head, he'd take off in the opposite direction, looking back over his shoulder to give me a saucy, screw-you grin. He wouldn't return until he was damn good and ready, by God.

The one surefire way to capture Mutt was to jump in my car and start the engine. He loved going for rides—that is, once he was over getting carsick.

Mutt was on the run one evening as Art and I were going out to dinner. As usual, we couldn't catch him. I tried hot dogs, a short rib, dog cookies without any luck. He gave me his ha-ha look and trotted off down the ditch. I gave up, got into Art's car, and we left. A couple of hours later, we were back. Art pulled into my driveway, his headlights illuminating my station wagon.

"What the hell is that?" Art said as two furry triangles rose up from the driver's seat.

"Oh, no, I must have left the window open. It's Mutt."

As I got out of Art's car, Mutt wriggled out the window of mine with a self-congratulatory smile.

"In his canine mind, he thinks he went for a drive," Art said.

Mrs. Kubler summoned Animal Control so often that I bet she had their number on her speed dial. If Mutt was off his line when Animal Control's truck headed for my house, I couldn't always get into my car fast enough. The fines for having an unleashed dog were hefty, plus they were incremental. Fortunately, the dogcatcher who came most of the time, Mr. Pacheco—Gene—was a nice guy. He couldn't catch Mutt either. After a while, he gave up trying. Nor did he write me tickets. If he thought Mrs. Kubler was watching, which she usually was, with her nose flattened against the glass of her bay window, he would doodle on his pad for a while, tear off the page authoritatively, and hand it to me with a conspiratorial smile. He would sit on my porch while we waited for the dog to materialize. On a hot day, Gene would have a glass of iced tea with me.

"You know what's the matter with your dog?" he said one afternoon.

"Yeah—everything," I said.

He laughed. "I'll bet you any money he's part coyote."

"Really?"

"Yup," Gene said. "Really. He's got the long nose, the big, perked up ears, the bushy tail, the reddish tinge to his fur. He's a coydog, probably a shepherd/coyote mix. Hate to tell you this—he'll never do what you want him to."

That told me why Mutt was ornery and stubborn, but it didn't tell me how to deal with him. Or with Mrs. Kubler.

I had to be extremely careful with my next-door neighbors. I was buying my house from them on a real estate contract, the only way I could afford my own place. I had initially gone to the bank seeking a mortgage. The loan officer took one look at me—a single, twenty-eight-year-old, $6 an hour silversmith—and my rather brief financial statement (I owned a $200 savings bond, a ten-year-old VW station

wagon, and five (5) shares in the Wendy's Corporation)—
and fell on the floor laughing.

After he stopped his guffawing, the banker told me he
couldn't loan me money for that house anyway because it
was "not suitable for investment."

Art, who was an insurance agent, explained the bank
had redlined the neighborhood. "Are you sure you want to
live there?" he asked me.

"Of course!" I said. "The house has a full grown pear
tree in the front yard. I love pears."

The Kublers were willing to give me a $16,500 contract
for the 900-square-foot house next door to them that probably had been officers' quarters for Kirtland Air Force Base
during World War II. I couldn't afford the $165 a month
payments, so Mr. Kubler—Ralph—lowered the payments to
$145 a month by giving me a longer contract. Under duress,
my mother loaned me $5,000 for the down payment, to be
paid back with interest. She even made me sign a notarized
IOU.

Never mind. I was thrilled to have my own home, hum-
ble as it was.

Crotchety Mrs. Kubler wasn't content yelling at me solely
for something my dog had done. "You stop chasing Mr.
Kubler around the cornfield and gossiping with him!" she
screeched at me more than once.

My social life has always been underwhelming, but I
wasn't that desperate. Ralph was at least eighty. He had
emphysema from his years of smoking Lucky Strikes and

working in the uranium mines near Grants. He wasn't chasing anybody anywhere, least of all me. Even as a lapsed jogger, I could outwalk his fastest run anytime. Granted, he was a nice man. Yes, I did talk to him out back in the cornfield once or twice. I asked his advice on caring for the fruit trees he had planted in my backyard and how to use ditch water to irrigate them. But honestly, we never stooped to gossiping.

Mrs. Kubler had Ralph thread slats of turquoise blue aluminum through the six-foot-high chain-link fence running between our lots. I guess the idea was to make it opaque, but the slats came loose in the wind. In no time, her turquoise aluminum Berlin Wall looked more like a shredded tin can. Plus the metal strips rattled in the faintest of breezes and kept me awake.

Mrs. Kubler wasn't finished protecting her swain from me. No doubt at her behest, Ralph built what looked like basketball backboards in front of each of my three windows facing their house. Since I didn't think either of them was taking up the game, I concluded this latest maneuver was to prevent me from spying on them. Or maybe to keep Ralph, who was legally blind, from spying on me, his new love interest, sex slave, and gossip partner.

I didn't dare leave Mutt inside during the day while I was at my job making silver jewelry in a small workshop near the university. I fastened him to the clothesline out back, in the shade of black walnut trees, with plenty of water, food, and something to gnaw on. He could easily slip his collar, and often did. I'd come home to find his empty collar lying in the grass, still attached by a cable to the clothesline. Had aliens abducted him? If so, they'd be sorry.

Where did Mutt go on his jaunts? Sometimes he went up onto the ditch bank to chase ground squirrels or, better yet, the postman's sly tomcat. Or he rolled in squished toads in the street. From friends who saw him cruising the neighborhood, I learned he was an expert dumpster diver, and the Furr's Supermarket dumpster on Fourth Street was one of his favorite haunts. Being an equal opportunity garbage hound, he also dived at the Safeway across the street.

I came home one afternoon to find his cable still fastened to the clothesline, but it led under Mrs. Kubler's chain-link barrier. I peeked through the slats. Mutt was on her side of the fence, snuggled up against the metal mesh, unable to move, whimpering, and looking mournful. There was no scooped out hole to indicate he'd dug under the chain-link, which was tight to ground level. His lead went under the fence, so clearly he couldn't have vaulted it. Needless to say, Mrs. Kubler, who hated Mutt as much as she despised me, had already called Animal Control. As I was trying to figure out this latest conundrum, an officer other than Gene showed up.

"Look, he's not running loose," I argued. "See? He's tied up."

The officer sided with Mrs. Kubler, who said my dog was trespassing on her property. I was out another $30. I have never figured out how Mutt ended up on her side of the fence.

If Mutt was loose, he liked to lie on the front lawn under the pear tree, where I left him an auxiliary water dish and food bowl. A crow began to visit his digs, sneaking pecks of food, dipping into his water. I knew it was the same bird because he had a crooked right leg and limped as he circled Mutt's camp in a proprietary waddle. Curiously, the dog never seemed to mind much, although he certainly objected if another dog or the postman's cat approached his provisions.

I saw the crow saunter up to Mutt with a stick in his beak. Mutt, who was resting his head on his paws, raised an eyebrow. The crow dropped the branch in front of him. Mutt picked up one end, the bird picked up the other, and they had a tug of war. Whenever the crow got the stick away from Mutt, he threw back his head and cawed victoriously.

The crow hung around most days. He even visited Mutt while he was tied up out back. I once saw him hop onto the dog's back and walk up and down his spine like a Thai masseuse. He and Mutt were quite a pair. Naturally, I called him Jeff.

Mutt was a year old when Stu sashayed into my life. He was a jewelry rep who sold Indian turquoise and silver at trade shows and to retail stores in the Southwest. He was especially successful with high-end galleries in Aspen, Jackson Hole, Santa Fe, LA, and New York. He liked our workshop's more contemporary line and repped it too. One day, he saw me polishing some ear cuffs of my own design.

"Well, what have we here?" he drawled.

I looked up from my buffer into Stu's gleaming malachite eyes with my gleaming lapis lazuli ones. "Oh, I'm just fooling around," I said.

"Yeah, maybe. These are extremely cool looking. I like the open work. Isn't it tricky to saw out something so small?"

"It is, but I use a new Dremel. I can't have the DTs if I'm going to do delicate work like this, or I'll screw up."

He laughed and picked up one of the finished cuffs. "I bet I could sell these for you," he said.

Did I imagine him batting his long, dark eyelashes at me when he said that? Was he leaning into my work a little closer than usual? Was he checking me out as much as he was checking out my silver? I had to wonder: Was this about ear cuffs—or me?

And I had to hope. This Marlboro man, in perfectly faded denim, was definitely sexy. Sun streaked hair shaded his forehead, curling at his neck beneath his ears. His cowboy body was tall and lean. His smile was laid back. His hands were long and strong, his fingers unmarred by a wedding band. The other silversmiths pretended they weren't listening to our conversation. But I knew they were hanging on to his every word and eyelash flutter.

I wanted to be careful. My boss, Greg, didn't mind me doing my own work on my own time with my own materials in his shop. He was likeable, fair, and he paid me well. Silversmiths were plentiful in Albuquerque. Good bench jobs were hard to find, especially for non-Indian art majors like me.

So in a low voice, I suggested to Stu we should get together to discuss it, but not on company time. I wasn't being sneaky—or so I told myself. "I'll be home about 5:30," I said and drew him a little map.

The minute he left, my coworkers teased me mightily.

"Wow, Gretchen," Lucy said. "You watch out for that hombre. Cowboys are heartbreakers. Two of my husbands were cowboys. I know what I'm talking about."

I drove my VW into my driveway at the appointed hour. Stu immediately pulled in behind me. He parked his shiny, stop-sign red, '58 Ford pickup and leaped out of the cab with a six-pack of Tecate.

I whipped up a bowl of guacamole. We sat on the porch, our legs dangling over the edge as we sipped beer and scooped up the dip with corn chips. Mutt was still tied up out back, putting up a terrible fuss. We could barely talk for the din. I was sure Mrs. Kubler's finger was twitching centimeters above the speed dial to Animal Control. I gave in, went to the backyard, and unchained the dog. He tore around to the front of the house and stood facing Stu, growling menacingly.

"I've never seen him like this," I said apologetically. "When my pals visit, he's usually friendly."

Unfazed, Stu dropped a few chips on the ground. Mutt stopped growling. He crept forward cautiously, snatched the food, backed up, and wolfed it down. Stu tossed more chips at Mutt's feet. He inhaled those, too. When no more fell to the ground, Mutt sat on his haunches, licked his chops, and waited. Stu stared intently into the dog's eyes for a long time until Mutt had to look away. Then he tossed the dog another handful of chips.

We decided to go out to dinner the next Saturday at the Mexican Carryout Kitchen on North Fourth Street, not far from my house. It was raining steadily that evening when Stu bounded up onto my porch promptly at six. I didn't have a doghouse for Mutt, so I decided to leave him inside. He had just made a big deposit on Mrs. Kubler's grass and peed on her tires, so I thought he'd be OK for a couple of hours. It was tricky getting out of the house without him slipping past me, but I made it. When I locked the door behind me, Mutt protested like crazy.

We had a delicious dinner at the Kitchen—their specialty, stuffed sopaipillas with red chile—accompanied by a long, pleasant, getting-to-know-you conversation. Not surprisingly, Stu had indeed grown up a cowboy, roping and riding on a cattle ranch in northwestern Colorado with a big, extended, mostly jack Mormon family of siblings, cousins, aunts, uncles, and grandparents.

"I rode the rodeo circuit for a while as a bulldogger," he told me. "Broke a lot of bones, got my head bashed in too many times. Then I wised up and went to college at Fort Lewis in Durango. I was two years into a degree in geology when it occurred to me that all the jobs for geologists were in Houston working for oil companies. I wanted no part of it, so I dropped out, and tried to make a career out of my sideline of selling Indian jewelry at rodeos.

"What about you? What's your story, Gretchen Maier?"

"I grew up in a mill town in Massachusetts with my

older sister and my widowed German Catholic mother, who barely speaks English. She's kind of sauer—that's German for 'cranky.' Not surprisingly, I was hot to leave home. At seventeen, I went as far away for college as I could go. After I got my degree in studio art from UNM, I stayed here."

"Gee," he said. "We have so much in common."

It had stopped raining by the time we closed down the Kitchen and headed home. Stu followed me up the steps onto the porch. I opened the front door a crack, hoping Mutt wouldn't escape. But the dog slammed past me, nearly knocking me down. Stu tried to snag his collar and missed.

"Damn!" he said. "That boy's slicker 'n snot!"

"It's OK," I said. "If he's been drinking out of the toilet like he usually does, he probably has to pee."

I turned up the living room lights. "Oh, my God," I said. Without looking in a mirror, I knew I was beet red.

Mutt had festooned the living room with the entire laundry basket of my dirty underwear. Bras hung from the arms of chairs, and my panties—most of them with stretched out elastic, worn thin and gray and full of holes— artfully adorned the floor. I thought I'd die.

Stu howled.

I promptly bought new underwear. Stu noticed.

He had an apartment in Denver, but he traveled a lot, going to gift shows, making calls on stores all over the West. He was in the Albuquerque area for a week or so each month, and he always stayed with me. We often went camping in the mountains on weekends. Mutt got so excited when he saw us putting camping gear in the pickup that he peed on his own feet.

The second we stopped at a campsite, Mutt would take off and be gone for hours. One time, he came back dragging a disgusting, chewed-on deer leg. On another outing, he returned to camp proudly sporting a ruff of fresh cow shit around his neck as green as a Christmas wreath. Stu grabbed Mutt like a rodeo calf, threw him to the ground, hogtied his legs together, and raised his arms in triumph.

"Record time!" I yelled.

We hauled buckets of water from the creek and poured them over a chagrined Mutt, who looked like a drowned rat. He was even more miffed because of the shampoo and rinse we gave him.

Inevitably, some of Mutt's regalia transferred itself to Stu's clothes. I drew another bucket from the stream and dumped it on him. He came up gasping from the cold water, snatched the bucket away from me, and gave me the same treatment. In no time, we were both soaked and shivering.

"I think we'd better get out of these wet duds at once," he said, unbuttoning my shirt. "Hell, you could get hypothermia any minute."

"You, too. Let me give you a hand," I offered, reaching for his salad plate size belt buckle.

Stu invited me to go with him on one of his road trips: Durango, Silverton, Telluride, Aspen, Vail. It was mid-June, too hot in Albuquerque, not much work at the shop, plus I had never been to Colorado. I was ready for a vacation.

With so many stops, I knew we couldn't take Mutt, so I called Art to see if he would be willing to look after him. "We'll be gone for maybe ten days."

"Well, I don't know. Do you think he'll come to me when I call him?"

"If you really need to catch him, hop into your car and turn it on. Remember that time we came back from dinner? He'll think you're taking him for a ride."

Colorado was green, cool, and beautiful, its mighty peaks still white with patches of snow, the skies clear and blue, the streams rushing with ice melt. While Stu called on customers, I hung out in a park or by a river, reading. In Aspen, we sat on the lawn outside the big tent where they held the Aspen Music Festival, listened to Schubert, ate pizza out of the box, and drank red wine from the bottle. It was a wonderful, relaxing vacation.

We arrived back at my place near dusk. Art was sitting on my porch drinking a lemonade. We joined him with our bottles of beer. The door to my house was open, no dog in sight.

"Where's Mutt?' I asked.

"Beats me," Art said. "That damn critter's been gone a lot. He's got everything he needs out by the clothesline—food, water, a Ferragamo pump. He takes off any time he wants to and returns home when he feels like it. The last time I saw him, yesterday afternoon, he was trotting down

Fourth Street, lifting his leg on each and every stick of furniture out in front of the antique shops. I was going to open my car door to call him. Then I thought, whoa! Those storekeepers are going to be pissed—so to speak. They'll take down my license number and come after me. He's not my dog, I reminded myself, so I left in a hurry. Sorry, Gretch'. I did my best."

"I know you did."

Art took a slug of his lemonade, which I suspected had a stiff snort of rum in it. Then he laughed. "Have I got a story for you."

"Lay it on me," I sighed.

Stu crossed his legs, propped his elbow on his knee, and grinned in anticipation.

"A day or two after you left, I decided to go to the dairy on Second Street to get milk. Mutt was loose, and since the Animal Control truck was coming down the street, I started my car, opened the back door, and hollered for him. He appeared out of nowhere and leaped into the back seat. His paws were muddy, and he smelled like something that had been dead for days, but, because I was planning on washing and vacuuming out my car later, I didn't mind too much. I drove to McIlhenny's with my window open so I could breathe. At the dairy, I rolled up the window, leaving it open maybe two inches for Mutt to get some air while I went into the store. Knowing I wasn't going to be more than a minute or three, I ignored Mutt's yelping. I came out to discover he was nowhere in sight. I can't believe he could slip through that tiny opening, but I guess he did."

"His middle name is Houdini," I said.

"Then I heard this horrible screeching coming from a white '65 Cadillac parked down from my Corona. In the front seat sat an elderly lady in a white silk shantung Chanel suit with a perfect, blond beehive hairdo and enormous fake gold and rhinestone jewelry. She was thrashing around and yelling bloody murder. In the backseat—white leather, no less—sat Mutt. He was perfectly calm and collected, looking for all the world like the Caddy was his own private limousine, like the hysterical woman in the front seat was an annoying interloper.

"I thought I'd die laughing. I knew he'd ignore me if I called him, and I certainly didn't want to identify myself as having anything to do with such a disgusting creature. If I drove away, maybe he'd follow me. I started the car and headed out of the parking lot. Sure enough, Mutt leaped into the front seat of the Caddy, bounded onto the lady's lap, and flew out her window.

"I drove down Second Street with two unforgettable images in my rearview mirror. One was the lady standing by her Caddy, still shrieking as she frantically tried to brush Mutt's mud off her shantung suit. And the other was Mutt, the Wonder Dog, tearing after me with his tongue hanging out the side of his mouth. I made him run a good, fast, half-mile before I pulled over to let him into my car for the rest of the trip home. I had no problem tying him up again. He was exhausted. I had to fill his water dish three times."

I shook my head. "What's a girl to do?"

Stu and I were what my mother would politely call be-freundet for several years. We saw each other on a regular basis, sometimes meeting up on the road. I didn't know what sort of future we had, but I was fairly sure he wasn't any more interested in marriage than I was. We were a perfect pair, easy with one another, laughing, joking, teasing, making hay.

Then one morning, my boss, Greg, came up to my bench with a funny look on his face and sat down on the stool next to me.

"Uh, oh," I thought. I immediately began to worry I was going to get laid off. Or fired. He had said it was OK with him for Stu to rep my earrings. Maybe now it wasn't OK.

"Uh, Carley and I decided at the last minute to go to the LA Gift Show last weekend," he said.

"How was it?" I asked.

"Crazy," Greg said. "Zillions of people, zillions of things, lots of glitter and jingle in the jewelry. Most of it was truly hideous, poorly made crap. The show was sort of fun, but it was overwhelming. Neither of us has any interest in ever going again."

He hesitated, and I became still more nervous. Here it comes, I thought, the lightning bolt. My job, my house, my car, my jewelry business, everything was going to go up in smoke.

"Stu was there. He had a booth."

"Yeah," I said. "I know. I offered to go help him for a couple of days. He said it would be too boring for me, a waste of my time."

Greg frowned. "Carley says I have to tell you."

"Tell me what?"

"He wasn't alone."

"Well, no. I think he said he was sharing the booth with a Chinese woman who reps jewelry and silk scarves from Thailand."

Greg cleared his throat. "They were very friendly with each other," he said, looking away. "They were staying in the same hotel we were." Always a man of few words, Greg got off the stool and walked out of the room.

I was blown away. I couldn't breathe. I couldn't swallow. I was determined not to cry in front of my coworkers. I put my tools away, cleaned off my bench, gathered up my purse and jacket, and headed home. As I drove, I started to remember things that had struck me as being a little off-key with Stu of late. He recently had suggested I shouldn't call his apartment in Denver.

"I've got this new long-distance deal," he said. "Let me pay for our gab fests." He still called, but not often.

We hadn't gone camping for more than a year. "I'm too old and busted up to sleep on the ground," he said. "Give me a big, soft, squishy hotel bed and room service. Then I'll be a happy camper."

He never asked me to go on the road with him anymore. He came to town less often, maybe only a day or two every couple of months instead of every few weeks.

I exploded in the middle of Lomas Boulevard. I slammed my hand so hard on the steering wheel that I broke the horn's chromed rim. I knew he was two-timing me. Or maybe three- or four-timing me. Maybe he had a babe in every port. I called him every foul name that's not in my

Living Webster's Encyclopedic Dictionary of the English Language.

I got out of my car and wobbled up the front steps to my house. Mutt came tearing down the ditch and ran up to me. He wagged his bushy tail a few times and smiled. When I didn't stroke his head and pat him and talk to him as usual, he must have guessed something was wrong. He nudged my hand with his nose and whimpered. Once inside, I fled into my bedroom, slamming the door behind me. I sobbed for hours. On the other side of the door, Mutt whined and sighed, scratching from time to time, wanting in.

Stu called a few nights later, uncommonly upbeat. "Hey, Babe, what's happening?" he said jauntily.

"No mucho," I mumbled.

"You don't sound too good. Are you OK?"

"No," I said.

"It's nothing too serious, is it? Hey, this'll cheer you up. I had an amazing show in LA. I wrote more orders than ever. I sold two dozen of your earrings to a fabulous gallery in Miami."

I didn't say anything.

"I'll be in town Tuesday. I hope you'll be feeling better by then."

I hung up without replying.

I sat on the porch with Mutt for our customary cocktail hour on Tuesday as dusk was falling. Sipping a rum and Coke, I waited for the descending sun to tinge the Sandias their characteristic watermelon pink. Mutt was lying under the pear tree, his head on his paws. From time to time, he lazily slurped from his water dish. Overhead, hundreds of crows flew by, squadron after squadron, cawing noisily as they streamed south to the zoo where they spent their evenings dining on elephant dung.

The familiar red pickup glided into the driveway. Stu sauntered toward us, all smiles. Mutt got up, stretched, walked up languidly, shoved his nose into Stu's crotch, and got a good whiff. Annoyed, Stu batted his muzzle away. Then Mutt lifted his leg on Stu's pants and peed.

"Hey!" he yelped angrily. "Fucking mutt," he said, glaring down at the large, stinky, wet spot on his pressed jeans.

I took another sip of my drink. "He's on to you, honey pie. And so am I. See that big Charmin box by my car? It's full of your crap. Take it and get the fuck out of my life. Now."

Stu gaped at me slack jawed, not moving for what seemed like an age. "Is this about Mei Mei?" he asked tersely. "Some friend that Greg is. I can explain everything."

"Don't bother. I'm not interested."

I cried on Art's shoulder for months. He was sympathetic. "Gretchen, honey," he said, "men are like buses—there'll be another one along in five minutes."

"That's not true," I said.

"Yeah," he said. "It's not true for me, either."

Art had finally come out of the closet, and his bus was worth the wait. His new boyfriend, Gianni, was half-Vietnamese, half-Italian, and 100 percent gorgeous. We became great pals. He was a fabulous cook with his own catering outfit. I helped him in the kitchen for his big parties and served the guests. I learned a lot from him in addition to making extra money from tips.

My friends Jim and Susan Bradford moved into the neighborhood a block down the ditch from me. They were fellow jewelers with a home-based business and two delightful children. I began to spend a lot of my free time with them. We had cookouts or went on easy hikes with the kids or watched TV together.

After I notified the stores that handled my jewelry that Stu wasn't my rep anymore, I found I could sell directly to them and didn't have to pay his commission. My jewelry sales grew. I was fast paying off my real estate contract with the Kublers.

Mutt and I took up jogging again, going for runs down the ditch every morning. He loved it. I lost weight and felt way better than I had in years.

Then I got back into photography, set up a dark room in my spare bedroom, entered my landscape shots in the New Mexico State Fair, and won an Honorable Mention.

I took a course on petroglyphs at UNM's Continuing Ed that mostly consisted of field trips to sites all over New Mexico. Because of park rules, I couldn't take Mutt with me, so I left him with the Bradfords or Art and Gianni.

My friends fixed me up with somebody now and then, although I wasn't really on the prowl. At least I wasn't crying over Stu any more. He was a louse, period. If a guy cheats on you once, he'll cheat on you again—that's my take on things.

———————

I crossed paths with Stu at the workshop several years after I kicked him out. I was able to say hello without crumbling like a month-old piece of birthday cake. He was still handsome in a weathered cowboy way, but I was long over him.

When I came back from a weekend trip to photograph petroglyphs at the tanks east of El Paso, I found Art sitting on my porch looking glum. "I think there's something wrong with Mutt. He's having a hard time lifting his leg to pee."

"Oh, how tragic," I said lightly. "That's his greatest joy in life—at the top of the list, even before rolling in cow shit or squished toads."

I took Mutt to the vet, and sure enough, he had a tumor. I was heartbroken, far more upset than I'd been about Stu.

Although I fed him liverwurst, ground chuck, and every dog's favorite chow, canned cat food, he continued to lose weight and grew weaker. When he quit eating altogether and could truly no longer lift his leg, Art offered to take him to the vet for me to have him put to sleep. "I know you'd do the same if it was my pet," he said.

The day they put Mutt down, I stayed home from work and cried myself back to sleep. In the early afternoon, a crow's clamorous, insistent cawing woke me. I went to the front window. Jeff was perched on a dry branch of my pear tree, squawking, beating his wings madly, glaring at me—or so it seemed. He kept up his angry yammer nonstop for hours and didn't shut up until darkness descended. Then he flapped off into the night, joining one of the squadrons heading for the zoo. I never saw him again.

I buried Mutt's ashes under the pear tree.

Late the next night, I heard someone trying to break into my house through a front window. I grabbed the machete I always kept by my bed—a little something I bought at a garage sale—and tore into the living room, roaring like a rampaging elephant, holding the machete high above my head.

Snake had jimmied the window open and was raising it. I charged at him. His jaw dropped, and his eyes went wide with horror. He let the window go just as I slammed the machete into the windowsill millimeters from his fingers.

Ten more points for our side!

Time to get a new dog.

5
τime circles

PART I The Rez

"So, Anna," Darcy said with a sneaky smile. "Are you and Harry Sarnoff lovers?"

Anna looked across the Formica café table at her friend and squirmed. "I didn't think you knew I was seeing him."

Darcy rolled her eyes as she fed another piece of zwieback to her baby daughter, who sat placidly on her lap, shedding mealy crumbs down the front of her puffy pink snowsuit. "Girlfriend, Albuquerque's still a small town. Everybody knows you're going out with him. You snare a cool gent, and it's not grist for the gossip mill?"

Anna casually flipped her straight, blond hair back from her face and tucked it behind her ears. "Really? You think Harry's cool?"

"Uh, yeah. Every one of your pals would love to get our fingers into that man's wonderful salt-and-pepper Jewish afro—including Pete. Why are you keeping such delightful news under wraps?"

Anna blushed and examined her fingernails, finding them badly in need of new polish. "I feel a little awkward. I mean, Irene and I are friends—well, we used to be friends, sort of, anyway. Their divorce isn't even final yet."

"Oh, nobody cares about that," Darcy said with a dismissive wave of her hand. "She's going out with my oldest brother, of all people. Remind me how you know the Sarnoffs."

Anna shrugged. "I met them in the late '80s, when I was dating Andy Mason. Did you ever meet him?"

"I think that was before Joe and I moved here. I heard he was movie star handsome."

"Not to mention self-centered and unreliable. Anyway, he was a med school classmate of Harry's. They formed an eating club."

"What's that?"

"It was sort of a controlled potluck. Except for terrific hole-in-the-wall Mexican eateries, Albuquerque's dining scene then was dismal: dry steak, baked potatoes, iceberg lettuce with mayonnaise, jug wines."

"Ugh."

"The club was wonderful. Worth putting up with Andy. We would decide on a theme—Moroccan, Szechwan, northern Italian—and each person would prepare part of the meal. The results were amazing: fabulous curries, tapas, exotic enchiladas, Mongolian hot pot. I must have gained ten pounds. Often we held our feeds at Harry and Irene's place in the North Valley, mostly because, unlike the rest of us, they had plates that matched."

"Oooh, you're making me hungry." Darcy grabbed the zwieback out of her daughter's hand and gnawed it, making growly lion sounds. The baby screwed up her face and was on the verge of crying when her mother handed the toast back to her and squeezed her affectionately. "My brother says Irene's still bitter about the divorce."

"They're both difficult people, one more crabby than the other. Harry says once their three daughters left home, their marriage went to hell. He blamed menopause."

"His or hers?" Darcy asked.

Anna laughed. "Good question. Probably a tossup."

Outside the window of the café where the two women sipped their coffee, cottonwood branches, laden with wet snow, formed a bower above an empty patio. The day was sunny, and the late spring snowfall was melting fast.

"One night maybe six months ago, more or less out of the blue, Harry called me. 'Irene has exiled me from our house and sent me to a motel,' he told me. 'We're getting a divorce.'

"This wasn't a complete surprise, but I was shocked when he told me I was the first person he called. I've always enjoyed his company, but I never thought we were especially close. What's he see in me?"

"Oh, please," Darcy scoffed. "You're a fabulous cook, you've got style, and you're smart—for a blonde."

"Wow. I should have you writing my personal ads."

"Seriously, why wouldn't he be interested in you?"

"He's twenty-five years older and maybe the top psychiatrist in the state. I'm a flunky in a hospital billing department."

Darcy groaned. "Give yourself a break, Anna. You just finished an MBA while working a full-time job, and you're planning to open your own store. Besides, you're hardly ever without some delicious man. None of your friends can keep up with you."

"Alas, eventually they turn out to be jerks. On the other hand, your husband is the coolest straight guy in New Mexico. Can we clone him?"

Darcy laughed. "Yeah, Joe's wonderful, that's true. And he's mine, all mine. Anyway, tell me more about you and Harry. I can't believe you've been holding out on me."

"We see each other a couple of nights a week for a concert or dinner at his new place. He bought a former hunting cabin in Tijeras Canyon and turned it into a bachelor crib. Hot tub. Maximum stereo. A Weber that looks like a Rolls-Royce. He's deep into grilling. In fact, I think he's really enjoying being single again. He and Irene got married in their early twenties when he was still in med school."

"And?"

"Oh, we listen to music, talk books and politics. Sip fabulous wine from his cellar. Soak in the hot tub under the stars. Sometimes he confides in me some of the uglier aspects of his breakup with Irene, which amazes me. I'm not a fellow shrink."

"You're empathetic, and he knows he can trust you."

"Anyway, OK, so Harry and I sleep together. But I wouldn't say we're lovers. He's . . . um, he's hesitant. I guess I'm a little cautious myself."

Darcy finished her coffee and glanced at her watch. "Damn! I gotta run. Just when you were getting to the good part." She pushed back her chair, picked up the baby, and balanced her on her hip. "I'm taking my parents to the doctor's. Mom and I think there's something wrong with Dad. He gets very mixed up and forgets things."

"Oooh, I'm sorry to hear that. You're dad's adorable, even if his jokes are corny. Hope it's nothing too serious. Keep me posted."

"I'm dying to hear more about you and Harry, but it'll have to wait, I guess. In the meantime, you be careful with that man, Ms. Anna, and stay tuned in to your inner skeptic, you hear?"

"I will, *Mother*. My radar's on and fully operational."

It occurred to Anna that she'd verbalized something to Darcy she hadn't admitted to herself: she and Harry were both tentative about their relationship.

"I'm not in love with Harry," she told her friends Pete and Ed over drinks. "Sure, he's not bad looking. He's worldly-wise, and maybe I'm a little in awe of him. But he does have a number of qualities that aren't that wonderful."

"Like what?" Pete asked.

"Sometimes he's awkward with people he doesn't know well."

"Who isn't?" Ed said. "Then again, the man would be so much better looking if he didn't stoop. It's like he's worried about being too tall and curls into himself, as if to protect his center. It totally spoils the lines of those expensive sweaters he wears."

"Really," Pete said. "If I could afford Missoni, I'll stand up proud and tall. Show off my pecs and broad shoulders."

Ed laughed. "Dream on, Mr. Pudgeball."

"His table manners are appalling, and he has the strangest eating habits," Anna said. "Most of the time, he eats nothing all day. Then at dinner, he wolfs down pounds of rich food. I've seen him eat loaves of bread, whole chickens, huge slabs of carne adovada, entire pints of Häagen Dazs. It's embarrassing to go out to eat with him sometimes."

"You'd never guess it by looking at him. He's thin as a flagpole. Lucky man to have such a metabolism," Ed said, patting his paunch.

"He runs ten miles a day to stay fit. But I have to wonder: why does he drive around the block countless times until he can park directly in front of where he's going—even the gym?"

"It's an Albuquerque thing," said Ed. "In this town, people loathe walking. Like in LA. Remember that when you pick out a place for your shop. Customers have to be able to park smack in front of your building, or they'll keep going. Which probably includes your dear Harry."

"So he's a man of many contradictions," Pete said. "And he's not your Mr. Right. But if you're serious about opening your shop, doll, maybe you need to be focusing your energies on that—rather than on Harry's neuroses. Which reminds me, the most adorable little adobe, next door to my house, is about to go on the market. I immediately thought of you. Plus it has a parking lot in front."

"Tell me more," Anna said. "Old Town's exactly where I'd like to be."

Anna drove to Harry's place in the East Mountains for a Saturday dinner. As she walked into the kitchen, he stopped peeling potatoes, put down his paring knife, wrapped his arms around her, and kissed her on the cheek.

"What's on the menu, chef?" she asked.

"Linzer torte."

"Oh, my favorite! Your best dessert—anybody's best dessert. Is that the main course?"

"Nope. Got a beef tenderloin on the Weber," he said. "With an apple, sage, and wild mushroom stuffing. Scalloped potatoes, grilled asparagus. Fabulous wine to go with it, a Gruet Pinot Noir."

"Ah, now we're drinking local. I thought you said New Mexico wines were terrible."

"Changed my mind," he said. "I went to a tasting at the winery the other day and was pleasantly surprised. Their Chardonnay's not bad either, although it's their Blanc de Noirs Champagne that wins them all those prizes."

They sat out on the porch after dinner sipping the last of the wine and enjoying a splendid view of the stars above the pines surrounding Harry's cabin.

"It's getting chilly out. How about a Courvoisier?"

"I'll pass," Anna said. "I've got a long drive home, and navigating downtown Albuquerque on a Saturday night, I'd better have my wits about me."

Harry grinned and drew her close. "Who says you're going home tonight?" he said, nuzzling her neck with his bushy moustache.

———————

Anna joined Harry for a symphony concert at Popejoy Hall that featured an all Elliott Carter program. She appreciated the profundity of the work, but the screechy violins set her teeth on edge.

Harry thoroughly enjoyed the concert. "A pleasant break from stodgy ol' Mozart," he said afterward as they crossed the street to the Frontier Restaurant for a late dinner.

Midway through their meal, he announced gleefully: "I've got great news." He slapped both palms on top of the table between them, rattling the salt and pepper shakers. A broad smile turned up the corners of his moustache. He swallowed a large chunk of his triple green chile cheeseburger and wiped a fistful of paper napkins across his mouth.

Anna looked up from her burger, getting ready to take a bite.

"Hope you won't be mad about this," he said, shoving a handful of fries into his mouth.

"Try me," Anna said with a cautious smile.

"You know that conference I went to in San Diego last weekend?"

Anna nodded as she bit into her burger.

"Well, I met this woman on the plane out. We really hit it off, had a wonderful time together."

Anna chewed slowly.

"Uh, I think we're really meant for each other. We plan to get married and maybe start a family."

Anna had difficulty swallowing. The burger had turned to sawdust in her mouth.

Harry blithely continued. "In a year or two, after Tessa

gets her master's in art therapy, I think I'll move to Minneapolis to be with her. She and two other women own a house together, and we'll all live there. I shouldn't have trouble getting a teaching position in Minneapolis or St. Paul. Or," he added with a grin, "maybe I'll just sit on a park bench and invite people to tell me their troubles."

Harry was beaming like a boy who'd batted a baseball out of the stadium.

Anna nearly choked. What was she supposed to say? "That's wonderful, Harry—I'm so happy for you."

Instead, she fumbled for words. "Uh, Harry, aren't you being a bit rash? You don't really know this woman."

He shrugged.

Anna drove home from the Frontier in a fog of confused emotions, not the least of which was anger. Although it was past midnight, she was too wound up to go to bed. She put on a CD of Zydeco music and cranked up the volume. Sipping a stronger than usual gin and tonic, she attacked her refrigerator, tossing out leftovers, limp vegetables, wrinkled fruit, and half empty condiment jars. The remains of Harry's prized Linzer torte hit her wastebasket with a resounding thump. She fixed herself another G&T and manically mopped her kitchen floor. At 3 a.m., she went to bed, still agitated, still thinking up all the well aimed barbs she could have pitched at Harry.

In hopes of falling asleep, she scanned a best-selling mystery. Five messy murders and a steamy lay for the protagoniste in the first twenty pages. She tossed the book into a corner, pulled the blankets up over her head, and fell into a numb slumber, her tongue puffy and dry from the alcohol.

She surprised herself by calling the hospital in the morning and saying she had the flu. This prevarication from Miss Perfect Attendance all through grade school? The girl who missed a single day of class in high school because of an emergency appendectomy? The dutiful, dependable employee who never called in sick?

Anna packed a knapsack and drove to the foot of the Sandias. In robust good health, she set out on La Luz Trail, which led seven miles up to Sandia Peak. The day was hot, dry, and summery, her hiking boots raising dust on the path. Her lungs protested as the mountain air became thinner, but three hours later, the main fork in the trail came into view. By then, her throat was raspy from the exertion, her knees ached, and sweat poured from under her cap, running down her face in dirty, salty rivulets. She felt lightheaded. But she balled her fists and shot them into the air. "I did it!" she yelled.

A quarter mile ahead, she sat on a cool stone wall, drank from her water bottle, and took in a spectacular birds-eye panorama of central New Mexico, a view worth every step, every drop of sweat. Below her limestone perch, a steeply pitched evergreen wilderness gave way to a broad, dry landscape encompassing hundreds of square miles of juniper and cedar dotted high desert. The plains were split by the green bordered brown ribbon of the Rio Grande flowing south, flashing its watery mirror in the midday sun. Looking up into the cloudless sky, she watched a pair of ravens twirl around each other like black crepe paper streamers. Suddenly, they folded their wings and, bullet like, plummeted toward earth. Moments before they crashed into the pines, they cawed with laughter, separated, and flew back into the sky to do it again. Overhead, the dark, sketchy dash of a solitary hawk rode thermals in wide circles as a white hot sun neared its apex. Soon it would begin to slide toward the dormant volcanoes that defined Albuquerque's western edge.

Anna sat quietly, letting her mind meander, taking in the silence of the mountain summit, interrupted now and then by the ethereal, flutelike call of a hermit thrush or the noisy play of stellar jays in the forest below.

"Gee," she thought to herself, "what am I doing up on top of this mountain in the fresh air and sunlight when I could be down in that dreary hospital basement with nonstop ringing telephones, the rattle of computer keys, and the nattering of my talkative coworkers? Wake up, Anna. See what a huge, gorgeous place the world is? It's far more compelling than Harry Sarnoff."

He called that evening while she was in the tub, soaking away her aches. "Still on for dinner Saturday?" he asked. "You seemed a little surprised by my news last night."

"Yes, I am surprised. You know, I need a few weeks to think things over."

"Really?" Harry said. "What's to think over? You know you mean a lot to me, our friendship, the time we spend together. This thing with Tessa doesn't change that. Hope we can still be friends. Besides, I'm not leaving for another year."

Harry called exactly three weeks later to invite Anna to dinner at his cabin. Surprising herself, she accepted. What the hell. If she were truly his friend, she had to be happy he'd found the woman of his dreams, didn't she?

Harry grilled steaks. "Think I'll open a bottle of '74 Heitz Martha's Vineyard Cabernet."

"Your prized vintage. What are we celebrating?"

Harry smiled.

Anna made a salad of cold, steamed vegetables and set a table on the porch. Harry filled their wineglasses, and they sat down.

"Here's to our enduring friendship," Harry said, raising his glass to her.

He slurped his wine. "Ah, fabulous. Say, how's life in the dungeon?" he asked, grasping his fork in his fist and jabbing it into his huge sirloin.

"It's unbearable." Anna cut off a bite-size piece of her petit filet. "If I have to tell one more person we're going to take her house if she can't pay for her gallbladder operation, I'll go postal. I'm counting the days till I'm out of there."

"You're going ahead with this store idea of yours?" Harry asked.

"Absolutely. Four more months, and I'm hospital history. I'm buying a wonderful little adobe next to my friend

Pete's house. You'll love it; it has parking right in front. We don't close until October 15, so the remodeling will have to happen quickly if I'm going to be open for Christmas. Refinish the floors, paint the walls off white. All the outside trim needs attention. But fortunately, the stucco is in good shape, and I like the buckskin shade. Next spring, I'll buy planters and put geraniums outside the front door to add color."

Harry shook his head. "Don't understand why you'd give up a secure job at the hospital for some pipe dream of yours, especially when your present employment provides you with a pension and health care."

Anna frowned. "Thanks for your support. I've been thinking about this for years and saving for it. Ever since I was a little kid, I dreamed of having my own store. Which is why I got my MBA, in fact. When I showed the bank my market analysis and business plan, they said it was the best commercial loan application they'd ever seen. They agree the location is super, and Albuquerque's ready for a store like mine."

"Hmm," Harry said, plunging back into his steak.

Harry talked about his new crop of psychiatry residents at the med school later that summer. "I'm taking them out to White Cliff Farms on the Navajo reservation in early October. Want to introduce them to Native American ways of dealing with mental health. We're going to camp out at the home of Dan Tom, a medicine man I worked with in the Indian Health Service."

"Oooh, how fascinating," Anna said. "Can I go along?"

Harry cleared his throat. Staring out into the dark, he ignored her question.

Anna was perplexed. Harry often invited her to gatherings with his residents. Why would this weekend be any different? Was she somehow being presumptuous? She fumbled for words. "Uh, well, I mean, if you think it's OK, that is."

Harry still said nothing.

"Is Tessa coming?"

"No. She has a term paper due." He thought for a while, then said, "Guess it's all right if you come."

Anna didn't care if Harry was being equivocal. She'd lived in New Mexico for fifteen years and knew that a weekend in Indian Country and a ceremonial were rare opportunities to learn more about life in the Navajo Nation.

Harry picked up Anna at her condo on a Friday afternoon. His Jeep Cherokee led a convoy of four vehicles heading west toward Navajo country, the land Harry referred to as "the rez." Anna sat up front, sharing snacks and lively chatter with him and several of his students in the back seat.

"Where ya from?" An auburn haired woman asked her.

"Originally? Northern Maine," Anna answered.

"No way. I'm from York. I thought I detected a bit of a Down East accent. I used to go to summer camp up north, almost on the Canadian border."

"Camp Wampompeag?"

"Hey, you know how to pronounce it. Yup, as a matter of fact. Don't tell me you went there, too?"

"Once, in 1985, when I was fourteen."

"Wow. Guess I was a couple of years behind you. We're the oldest people on the trip, except for the professor."

"Genuine antique," Harry said proudly.

"I'm Joan Timmerman," she said, reaching her hand over the front seat to shake Anna's.

"Oh, sorry," Harry said. "Introductions. Anna Gaudet, a friend from the hospital. The fellow sitting behind me is Ron Coriz, from Santo Domingo Pueblo. And the curly haired young lady in the middle is Ginny Swenson."

"Papa's star pupil," Ron Coriz muttered under his breath.

The sun began to slip from view behind a limitless, rolling backdrop of cedars, junipers, and piñón trees. Harry turned off the highway onto a rutted track of baked clay. As they bounced down the road, he jerked the steering wheel this way and that in a vain effort to avoid potholes. The car seats' springs squealed, and the riders laughed good-naturedly as they were tossed about like tennis balls.

"Part of the fun of life on the rez," Harry said.

After a couple of miles, the road dead-ended where the neat forms of a small, Navajo homestead—several log hogans, a tar-papered house, corrals, and a cornfield—were clustered at the base of white cliffs now tinged vermilion in the late afternoon light. The sky was streaked with lavender contrails and wispy clouds. Harry stopped the Jeep in front of the small house, and the other vehicles followed suit. He motioned to the passengers to stay put. In a hushed tone, he said, "Now we wait. Navajos consider it impolite to get out of your car before you're welcomed by a family member."

A weathered, white haired Navajo man came out of the house, dressed in cowboy clothes: faded jeans, a snap button blue shirt, worn hat and boots the same shade of dust as the earth. When he gestured for everyone to get out of their cars, Harry jumped down and called out, "Yah tah hey!" his snappy version of a Navajo greeting. Striding up to the medicine man, he grasped his hand, gave it a pump-handle shake, threw an arm around the Navajo's shoulders, and hugged him.

Anna was surprised. Maybe hugs and firm handshakes were the thing to do in the Anglo world, but Harry's manner seemed contrary to the Native Americans' more circumspect and gentle greetings she'd observed during her years at the hospital. "Remember, Harry isn't smooth socially," she reminded herself.

While the old friends conversed quietly, Anna and the rest of the passengers stretched their cramped muscles. Altogether, there were some fifteen fit-looking men and women in their twenties. Unsure of proper rez etiquette, they stood in a cluster, awaiting instructions from their host, Dan Tom, who spoke to them in staccato, uninflected English that told Anna it wasn't his first language. He introduced himself in the time-honored Navajo manner, naming his mother's clans and his born-to father's clans, welcoming everyone to White Cliff Farms as he circled the group lightly touching each visitor's hand in a gentle, polite greeting.

"I hope this weekend will be helpful to you in understanding some of the ways we Indians traditionally handle personal problems and mental illness. We're going to have a ceremony for a young woman who's having difficulties with her family. She's Spanish and Indian both, from northern New Mexico, and her parents have asked me to do this for her. I'm what's known as a Roadman in the Native American Church."

The group followed Dan Tom to a mound of folded white canvas and a pile of peeled aspen poles in the center of a flat patch of ground. "First, we put up this tepee I made. Making tepees is part of how I earn my living, and I go everyplace with them. They're Plains Indians structures, not part of the Navajo way, but they're useful for our gatherings."

He explained how the tepee was constructed and how to put it up. "One person could do this in maybe an hour, if he had to. But today, I have all this strong, young help."

Several med students volunteered, and they erected the tepee in no time. It was thirty feet in diameter at its base and twenty feet tall, magnificent, majestic.

Anna joined residents ferrying flats of soda pop and boxes laden with loaves of bread, frozen turkeys, oranges, watermelons, vegetables, and paper supplies from the vehicles to the kitchen in the house. After they deposited everything on the counters, Mrs. Tom appeared. She was a trim, small Pueblo woman in jeans who laughingly shooed the visitors away. "You're tracking up my kitchen. Out! Out!" she said.

Evicted from the kitchen, Anna and the others fetched their belongings from the cars and bustled around inside the tepee, laying out their bedrolls. They stopped to watch as Dan Tom carefully built a log fire in the center of the tepee and adjusted the opening at the apex, so smoke would flow smoothly into the descending dark.

Ginny, Harry's blond mopped student, arranged her bedroll next to his, singing a little song to herself in a tinkling, breathy soprano. With her tiny body and dainty hands, she reminded Anna of a kindergartner.

Anna rolled out her foam pad and sleeping bag on Harry's other side, but she saw him scowl at her. She stopped what she was doing and sat back on her heels. "Is anything wrong?" she asked.

His turned his back on her and said nothing.

"Harry, I asked if anything's wrong."

He abruptly got to his feet, and without so much as looking at her, he joined a group of residents chatting on the opposite side of the tepee.

Anna was stunned. She felt humiliated in front of Ginny and the others. With the last light of day guiding her, she walked away from the tepee to the base of the cliffs. She rested her back against a smooth, flat sided rock still slightly warm from the sun and sighed. "What is with Harry? Why isn't he speaking to me all of a sudden?" she wondered.

She watched the yellow cone of the tepee glowing magically in the dark, with giant silhouettes moving inside. "Huh," she concluded, "I guess this is one more note failing to sound on the warped keyboard of our relationship. I suppose I could stomp into the tepee and embarrass him in return. Have it out with him in front of everybody, demand his car keys, and blow out of this place. That'd show him."

But Anna wasn't a drama queen; it wasn't her style. "Fuck Harry," she said to herself. "Ignore the bastard. Enjoy the ceremony you came here to experience."

The ivory canvas triangle, anchored to the earth and golden bright against an indigo sky, was a heart stopping sight, a terrestrial cousin to the harvest moon that inched its way up above the cliffs, illuminating the entire farmstead in a pale blue opalescence. A chill settled over Anna. It wasn't the cooling night air giving her shivers but the sense of being in a timeless, unique place.

A drumbeat thundered across the little valley, bouncing off the rock-walled escarpment behind her, signaling the beginning of the evening's ceremonial. She slipped inside the tepee and settled herself on the bare ground opposite the medicine man. Harry looked through her. Anna returned his empty gaze.

Around the tepee's perimeter, Indians, Hispanos, and the med students sat quietly, staring into the fire. The Navajo women, their hair pulled back in neat chignons, wore traditional finery—long broomstick skirts, velvet blouses, concho belts, heavy silver squash blossom necklaces weighty with turquoise, wide silver bracelets. Many of the men wore Navajo silver bolo ties, rings, and bow guards.

Pearl, the twelve-year-old girl who was the focus of the ceremony, was accompanied by a cousin her age. They sat side by side on a rug facing the medicine man, their heads together, nervously clutching each other. Anna noticed the contrast between Pearl's auburn curls and her cousin's straight, black hair. But she could see they were related, with oval, warm brown faces, and high cheekbones framing their dark eyes. Both of them wore pink stretch pants, and the rhinestones on their pastel sweatshirts glittered in the firelight.

The Roadman looked around the tent, calling the assembly to attention. His voice was low and rich. Speaking slowly, softly, he addressed the girls. Behind them, flames licked at the neatly laid logs of his fire.

"I hear you're having problems with your family, and at school, and with your parish priest as well," Dan Tom said. "Conflicts, confusion, and misunderstandings between a young person and the adults around her are normal at your age. You're leaving behind your childhood and becoming women. To make this important transition, you need support from all the people in your life—your friends, your schoolmates, your parents, your brothers and sisters, your cousins, and your community. Even though some of these people you see tonight are strangers, they care about you. They came here to share your difficulties and show their concern for your welfare.

"As everyone in this sacred circle can tell you, we adults have had to deal with most of the things that are now causing you such grief. We want to use our experience to help you through your passage into adulthood."

The cousins stared intently at the bare ground between Dan Tom and themselves as he lit a fat, loosely rolled cigar of Indian tobacco and puffed on it until it was burning smoothly, releasing a cloud of fragrant smoke. He whisked an eagle feather fan around the girls and let the feathers rest on each one's head. Then he passed the cigar to them.

They giggled shyly, bravely drew on it, and, choking a bit, enveloped themselves in more smoke.

Dan Tom spoke to the crowd. "Share this smoke with these young women and send them your good wishes for their happiness," he said. As each person took a puff and passed the cigar around the circle, the medicine man chanted in undulating, high-pitched Navajo and prayed, brushing the cousins lightly with his feather fan. The girls held each other, tears running down their flushed cheeks and dripping onto their sweatshirts.

The mood enhancing tobacco, the fire's hypnotic magic, the full moon's brightness penetrating the thick canvas, and the heartbeat of Dan Tom's drum were mesmerizing.

Gradually, the October night grew cold, as the fire died to a few burning log ends. Anna couldn't keep her eyes open, though she wanted to stay awake. She moved to her sleeping bag and burrowed into it. Harry and Ginny lay facing each other, whispering quietly "Sleep tight!" Anna whispered cheerfully to Harry's back. She wasn't surprised when he didn't reply. But Ginny's thin, milky white arm rose up above the mound of his shoulders, and she wiggled her fingers at Anna in a little girl's nighty-night wave.

Anna lay in a dreamy, hypnagogic state for a long time, enveloped in the steady drumbeat with which Dan Tom accompanied his subdued chanting. Through half shuttered eyes, she watched flames play over the logs and drifted effortlessly into sleep.

Sometime during the night, she was awakened by movement next to her. Opening one eye, she watched Harry struggle out of his sleeping bag and toss a couple of large logs onto the fire. They collided noisily, sparks flew in all directions, and flames leaped into the air. As he climbed back into his makeshift bed, Anna heard someone grunt. Dan Tom, still awake, still sitting cross-legged, shook his head, arose, and with a stick, carefully rearranged the burning logs into the neat quadrangle he'd maintained throughout his vigil.

Dawn seeped through the thick canvas, the med students began to stir, and Anna opened her eyes to find Dan Tom was no longer there. The fire had dissolved into tiny pyramids of ash, with a thin curlicue of smoke rising from the remaining embers. The girls and their families were gone, as were all the other Indians. Anna slid out of her sleeping bag, stretched, and ducked out of the tepee into a crisp fall morning. Already, the sun was steadily warming the earth, dispelling the evening's chill. A light ground fog gradually evanesced into a deepening, turquoise blue sky.

Her Native hosts had evidently been up awhile. Scents of coffee and bacon drew Anna toward the house. Through the open door, she saw Mrs. Tom and the other Indian women loading platters with steaming mounds of scrambled eggs, fried potatoes, pancakes, and bacon, placing them on the kitchen counter next to bowls of red chile and pitchers of syrup. Breakfast wasn't quite ready, so Anna visited the outhouse and washed up in one of the metal basins set on stumps beneath a cottonwood.

She returned to an animated line of visitors streaming

from the kitchen doorway. They slapped their empty paper plates against their thighs, laughing and chatting until Dan Tom rang the dinner bell. Harry was the first in line and emerged from the house, stuffing bacon into his mouth, his plate heaped with half a dozen pancakes.

"Kosher bacon?" Anna laughed to herself. She opted to wait until the queue thinned out and sat on the bumper of a pickup, lifting her face to the morning sun. The air was clean edged, refreshing, and fragrant with drying cottonwood leaves, sage, and burning piñón. Above the cliffs, enormous ravens circled, cawing loudly, as if demanding to be fed too.

After breakfast, she saw several med students follow Dan Tom into a sheep pen behind the house. "What's up?" she asked Joan.

"Lunch," she replied cheerily. "We're going to slaughter a sheep and make sausage. Aren't you coming?"

"Thanks, but no thanks," Anna said. "This is where I am magically and instantaneously transformed into a vegan. Surely you med students are less squeamish than I am about slitting a sheep's throat."

"Aww, don't be a wimp," Joan said.

"I am a devout and practicing wimp—a paper pusher. I file, therefore I am. Mrs. Tom hinted she could use help harvesting her corn. That sounds more appealing to me."

Anna waded into the cornfield off to one side of the house. From different directions she could hear the rustling of the dry stalks and the snap of people picking corn. "Mrs. Tom?" she called out.

"I'm here," the older woman replied from a few rows inside the corn patch.

Anna followed Mrs. Tom's voice and made out her blue kerchief and long sleeve red shirt in the stand of tall, faded brown plants. "Hi, I'm Anna."

"Please call me Bernarda, OK?" she said.

"Sure. How do I do this?"

"Break the ears off the stalks, leaves and all," she said. "Like this." She deftly snapped off an ear, then pulled back the leaves, exposing the kernels, and dropped the corn into a blue plastic laundry basket. "We peel them back so the corn won't get moldy and can dry properly. Maybe later we can use the husks for tamales." She handed Anna an empty basket. "There you go. When it's full, toss the ears into the bed of my pickup."

Anna and the rest of the Anglo corn picker contingent discovered that hand harvesting corn was hard work. She also understood why Bernarda wore a long sleeve shirt. The dry leaves of the stalks sliced her arms, and her face, too, if she wasn't careful. The dust in the field made her sneeze. But Anna found the work invigorating. The fall air was cool, and the sun warmed her shoulders and face. She became faster at snapping off the ears and in no time trundled her full basket to the pickup, where she dumped her load.

"You're good at this," Bernarda said when she returned to their part of the patch. "Are you sure you're not Native American?"

"A little bit. My mother's father was Pasamaquoddy, but he never got us on the tribal rolls."

"Too bad," Bernarda said. "You could be heir to a chunk of Maine."

Bernarda was chatty, unlike most of the Indian women Anna knew from the hospital. "Tell me about yourself," she said. "You're not one of the med students, are you? You're the doc's friend?"

"Uh, yes."

"Harry and my husband go way back. They used to travel together a lot on Indian Health Service business. That man of mine, he's always on the move," Bernarda said as she broke ears of corn off their stalks. "Those Navajos are nomads. Dan Tom doesn't stay in one place more than three weeks before he's off somewhere. It's in the blood. Now we Pueblo people are different. We stay put."

"Which pueblo are you from?"

"San Felipe. After I finished my doctorate at UNM, I got an offer to become assistant principal at the high school in Gallup. It was a splendid opportunity, one I couldn't turn down. There are still only a handful of us Native American administrators in the state school system. Taking the job meant I had to leave San Felipe, but the rez wasn't too far away, and the school let me go home for feast days. I met Dan Tom in Gallup. He was teaching math and coaching boys' basketball at our school. He's retired now. I'm due to retire next year. I can't wait."

"Are you going to hit the road with your husband?"

"Lord, no. The reason we're still together is because we're apart a lot of the time. No, I'm a homebody. I'm looking forward to spending more time at home in Gallup with my grandchildren and my rose garden. I guess it was that early Indian boarding school experience that makes me want to stay home as much as I can later on in life."

"I hope you don't mind my asking, but was it as bad as everyone says?"

Bernarda stopped picking corn for a moment. "Honey, I don't mind telling you it was awful. When I was seven, they took me kicking and screaming away from my family and my home and interned me in the Santa Fe Indian School. It was like jail. A lot of those teachers were mean as rattlesnakes when they come out of their holes in spring. We were forbidden to speak our own language, and if we did, they hit us over the head with a ruler or washed out our mouths with soap. They didn't ever allow us to go home except on major holidays. Not our holidays—theirs. I cried myself to sleep for months, but I never let those teachers see me cry. There we were, a mere forty miles from our parents, our grandparents, our aunties and uncles, our homes, our traditions, our language, but with no way to get there."

The other corn pickers overheard the discussion and peppered Bernarda with questions. "You Anglos have a habit of being too nosy," she laughed. "Let's just say it was cruel and unusual punishment to take Indians' children away from them," she said, turning on her heel and walking toward the truck with a basket of corn.

Anna rode with Bernarda to a hogan the family used as a makeshift granary, while the others returned to the house to wash up before lunch.

"So you're pals with Harry," Bernarda said as she drove.

With pursed lips, she nodded toward a rise where he and Ginny were slowly walking among the low walls of a rock and adobe ruin with their heads down. Occasionally, they'd stoop to pick up something and then stand close to each other to examine what they'd found. Anna guessed they were hunting for potshards or arrowheads. Ginny's fluffy platinum curls ringed her head like a halo, while the breeze batted Harry's afro about as if it were a tumbleweed. When he kissed her, Bernarda turned to Anna to watch her reaction.

"That man sure is something," she laughed. "I've known him for more than twenty years. I never thought he and Irene were very happy together. He always had something going on the side. And maybe she did, too."

Anna was shocked. "You mean Harry fooled around?"

"Uh-huh," Bernarda said. "The younger, the better."

Anna did her best to show no emotion, although her watery eyes betrayed her. She sniffled and took out a Kleenex to dab at her face. "Boy, this dust really is getting to me," she muttered.

Bernarda slowed the truck, put her arm around Anna's shoulder, and gave her a squeeze. "Honey, don't get me wrong, but that man's trouble. You can do a lot better, trust me. I love him, he's a well respected doc, he helps people. But he truly cares about one person, and that's Harry Sarnoff. Everybody realizes that sooner or later."

They unloaded the truck at the hogan, tossing the ears in through the doorway until long after the dinner bell rang. When the pickup was empty, Bernarda sorted through the pile for certain ears she had set aside. Instinctively, Anna wanted to ask her why, but she stopped herself.

Bernarda paused and looked up with a wry grin. "Don't you want to know why I'm picking out special ones?"

"Of course. But I'm trying to learn Indian manners."

Bernarda laughed and offered an armful of multicolored ears to Anna. "These are for you," she said. "Blue corn is sacred to us. And these others, like the pink and red speckled ones, well, I think they're beautiful. Keep the kernels in a dry place, like in a canning jar, where no bugs or mice can get at them, and plant them next spring," she said. "It's San Felipe corn. The best, of course."

"Thank you," Anna said. Smiling, she got into the pickup with her armload of corn.

The two women were the last to arrive for lunch, but there was still plenty of food. The wind had come up so the meal was laid out inside the house. Beds and chairs had been pushed against the wall, and a long, oilcloth covered plank table sagged under a load of turkey, stuffing, mashed potatoes, corn, biscuits, fry bread, gravy, fresh mutton sausage, salad, watermelon, and several kinds of pie. Farm food, Anna thought, a feast not unlike a Thanksgiving back in Maine.

Anna helped cleanup after lunch, then wandered into the tepee and collapsed on her bedroll for a siesta. Most of the group did likewise, though Harry and his little friend were absent. Anna lay in half slumber, gazing up through the smoke hole to a patch of intense blue sky streaked with feathery clouds. Mare's tails, Bernarda called them. Flies buzzed in the shaft of sunlight illuminating the fire pit below. Anna was asleep in a flash.

A distant drumbeat reverberating through the dirt floor woke her. Its pounding bass was like a heartbeat, threaded with Dan Tom's high register, hypnotic wail. Near the base of the chalky cliffs, the medicine man had covered a frame of bent willow branches with canvas to form a low, domed sweat lodge where the men converged.

The women gathered outside the tepee. "We're going for a walk," Joan told Anna. "Wanna join us?"

"Sure," she said. "Maybe it'll ease the soreness I'm feeling from picking corn and sleeping on the ground. I feel like I've gone twenty rounds with Sonny Liston."

"You, too?" Joan said. "I ache all over."

They strolled away from the farm through an arroyo below the cliffs.

"Do you believe these flowers?" Anna asked no one in particular. A profusion of fall blooms colored the hillsides: purple asters, goldenrod, orangey red Indian paintbrush, large mounds of dusty yellow chamisa, and masses of sunflowers, some tall and gangly, some small and delicate.

A hummingbird darted low above one woman's head, forcing her to duck.

"Hey, Shirley, he likes your red shirt," Joan said. "He thinks you're lunch."

The hummingbird, its wings a blur of violet and emerald green motion, zipped toward Ginny, paused to inspect her bright pink sweatshirt, then shot toward a flowering sage. The women watched as the bird, stopping and starting, poked its pointed bill into one flower after another. Suddenly, it buzzed up the cliffs and disappeared into the cedars and junipers above them, lost to human sight in the high reaches of a crystalline sky.

Anna noticed the other women seemed to shun Ginny. "Maybe it's because she's teacher's pet," she thought. Part of her enjoyed seeing them ignore Harry's girlfriend. But at the intersection of one arroyo with another, Ginny was about to trip over a flat clump of circular cacti when Anna grabbed her arm just in time.

"Thank you," the young woman said. Stooping to inspect the bluish plant hugging the ground like large blue green pincushions, she gasped. "*Lophophora williamsii.*"

"Huh?" Joan said.

"Peyote," Ginny said. "Wow! I've never seen it in the wild, only in pictures."

"What's the big deal about peyote?" Shirley asked.

"It's an hallucinogen used by Indians of the Southwest and northwest Mexico, primarily the Huichol," Ginny explained. "Members of the Native American Church sometimes use it ceremonially."

"How?"

"I'm told they eat it, and it makes them violently ill. But after they're through barfing, they see fabulous colors and have visions that guide them spiritually. Cool, huh?"

"Eeew, gross," Shirley exclaimed. "That's not the kinda church I grew up in."

"What kind was that?" Ginny asked.

"I was raised Pentecostal."

"Huh," Ginny said. "Let me guess—you spoke in tongues and handled rattlesnakes, didn't you?"

"People, please," Joan said. "A little respect, OK?"

The women returned from their walk as their male colleagues were coming out of the sweat lodge, their naked bodies gleaming in the afternoon light. Using gourd dippers, they splashed water from a fifty-five-gallon drum over themselves, dried off with towels, put their clothes back on, and wandered off. Several of the women noticed Harry leaving the sweat lodge after the others, wearing a pair of orange nylon swimming trunks. They nudged each other and giggled.

Dan Tom motioned the women over to the sweat lodge. He explained the procedure then sat on a boulder facing away from them as the women peeled off their clothes and crawled into the low roofed hut. The six of them sat shoulder to shoulder around a sunken pit of heated lava rocks glowing red and gray in the center of the packed earth floor. In the dim light afforded by the smoke hole in the roof, Anna saw Joan dip her fingers into a bowl next to the fire pit and flick water onto the glowing rocks, which hissed and released a hot fog.

Dan Tom's hand parted the flap of cloth that served as the door and passed in a lit cigar of Indian tobacco. "Share this and your good thoughts for one another along with it," he said. "I'll be outside praying for you."

Each woman puffed on the fat cigar before passing it to the next, and more smoke joined the steam in a cloud that erased all but faint shadows of their limbs—a hand, a leg, an arm. When it had burned down to a nubbin, Joan shredded it, sprinkling the remaining leaves on the rocks, where they curled up and burned into an aromatic haze.

Outside, Dan Tom sang an eerie, plaintive chant that rose and fell and swirled through Anna's head, as the pounding of his drum resounded in her chest and vibrated through the soles of her bare feet against the dirt floor. She drew the sage scented air deep into her lungs. Moisture began to stream from her forehead, dripping off her chin, sliding between her breasts and down her ribs. Water gathered on the ends of her hair and dripped onto her shoulders and arms. She found tears were streaming down her face. Soon her whole body was bathed in oily sweat, and her lungs were heavy with vapor.

She felt herself dissolving, becoming incorporated into a commonality like she'd never experienced. She heard sniffling and sighs, sounds that might have come from herself. Her heart was beating in time to the drum.

Joan started to sing, her melodious soprano blending easily with Dan Tom's voice. Everyone joined in. The song lasted a long time and flowed into others, until Joan began to cough. "I can't sing any more," she laughed. "I think I've sweated out all my tunes." She sprinkled more water on the rocks, and a wet cloud formed that showered the gathering with a fine mist.

The atmosphere in the small space was meditative. Self-consciously at first, the women shared their thoughts while staring into the pile of smoldering rocks.

"I don't know how you feel," Anna said, "but the ceremony last night was awe inspiring. I can't stop thinking about it."

"Me, too," Shirley said. "It made me reflect on my own adolescence, how awful it was a lot of the time, and how alone I felt, with nobody supporting me through it."

Joan said, "Dan Tom's approach to those girls was so sensible, so honorable, so respectful. What struck me was the realization that tribal people focus attention on their young people, celebrating and honoring their passage into adulthood with special rites and customs. Our so-called advanced societies deride the tribal world as 'backward' or 'primitive,' even 'savage.' But we often treat our teenagers with shame and derision. If that isn't savage, I don't know what is."

Joan spoke again. "I'd like to bring something up. I hope nobody minds if I say this, but I wish we residents would get along better. I think we've been a little testy with each other, jealous, too competitive, the women as much as the men. Maybe this is natural. We're a group that's recently come together, and we're under a lot of pressure to succeed. Believe me, I'm as guilty as anyone."

She turned to Ginny, who sat next to her. "I want to apologize especially to you. I haven't been as helpful as I could be, and I feel bad about it."

Others followed Joan's lead and told Ginny they were sorry for mistreating her.

In the half light, Anna saw that Ginny's eyes glistened.

Anna suddenly felt her lungs were sodden, the heat was closing her nostrils, and she was having trouble breathing. In a near panic, she crawled out of the hut and stood up. The others followed her outside, where they gulped down the cool, dry air and blinked to adjust their eyes to the blinding sunlight. Using the gourd scoops floating on the surface of the water barrel, they poured icy water over their heads and bodies, splashing one another playfully, naked and giggling like water sprites.

Anna found the cold water a blessing on her hot, sweaty body despite the sharp chill of the autumn afternoon. Her rosy skin felt rubbery, more taut and alive than ever before. She showered Ginny's head and shoulders with a gentle stream.

The younger woman wiggled with delight. "Oooooh, that feels wonderful."

The gourd slipped out of Anna's hand. When she bent to retrieve it, a white stone glinted in the sand at her feet. She picked it up and brought it to eye level, where she recognized the ivory flint as a perfectly knapped arrowhead several inches long. She ran a finger along its sharp edges.

"Look what I found!" she yelped.

The women gathered around her outstretched palm. Joan turned the arrowhead over in her hand. "Flawless. I've never seen such a beautiful point. Wow. What a treasure!"

Anna went looking for Dan Tom and found him inside the tepee, laying logs in a square for the evening's fire. "I've got something for you," she said excitedly and handed him the arrowhead.

He took it and examined it carefully. A little smile turned up the corners of his mouth, and he gave her a cheerful, sidelong glance. "Hmmmm," he said. "Beautiful."

Then and there, Anna was certain he'd planted the flint in the dirt beside the oil drum where one of the visitors was sure to see it.

He tried to hand it back to her, but she put her palms up. "No," she said. "It's yours."

He looked at her quizzically.

"This is your homeland, not mine. It belongs to you."

Dan Tom smiled with his whole face and slipped the arrowhead into his pocket.

Ordinarily, Anna would have cherished that arrowhead and kept it forever. It was the only complete one she'd ever found, and it was lovely. Yet even if Dan Tom hadn't planted it, she knew White Cliff Farms was his ancestral home, and taking it would be like swiping a family heirloom from his house. Besides, if this was his test—of Anglo materialism or respect for Indian manners or whatever else—she hadn't flunked. She felt good about that.

On the drive back to Albuquerque the next day, Ginny rode in the front seat next to Harry; Anna sat in back. As soon as White Cliff Farms and Dan Tom's tepee receded from the Jeep's rearview mirror, Harry began to chat as if nothing had happened. "It's like somebody flipped a switch," Anna thought. When she didn't answer a direct question he tossed over the back of his seat, she caught him looking at her quizzically in his rearview mirror. "OK, Harry, baby," she thought. "Both of us have on/off buttons."

It was easy to ignore him and the residents as they headed east toward home. The high desert landscape was far more captivating than their talk of football, university politics, the governor's race. The afternoon colors were brilliant, the highway a gray corridor between borders of abundant yellow, lavender, and white wildflowers. Rays of sunlight through the delicate purple asters rendered them almost luminescent. The hillsides and red cliffs near Gallup were suffused with the golden light that always meant autumn to Anna.

They arrived in Albuquerque as evening fell. Anna's condo was Harry's first stop. In silence, he helped her unload her gear from the Jeep and set it on her porch. Then he stopped and looked at her expectantly.

She faced him squarely. "I don't ever want to see you or hear from you again," she said in a flat voice.

"OK," he said. He backed away from her, got into his Jeep, and carefully reversed out of her driveway.

Anna opened her store within six weeks, just in time for the Christmas season. The renovations had been hasty. Her friends helped, especially Pete, Ed, Darcy, and Joe. The once grubby adobe sparkled with new paint, oiled vigas, waxed floors, and a wide variety of handsome, mostly handmade household furnishings from everywhere. She and her worker bees held a celebration, complete with champagne.

"Don't you dare spill anything on my beautiful floor," Anna warned her guests.

"Are you kidding?" Joe said. "I don't want to refinish that puppy a second time." He raised his champagne glass. "A toast to Anna and her gorgeous new store."

Anna lifted her glass. "Here's to my fabulous friends who helped make it happen."

Anna developed a morning routine: she arrived a few minutes before opening time, turned on the lights, raised the rice paper blinds, and neatened the piles of brightly colored fabrics and pillows. She flicked a feather duster over the glass shelves of étagères full of Japanese pottery, Czech crystal, and hand carved teak bowls from Thailand. At the desk, she made sure she had change, and that her receipt book and a pen were handy.

One midweek day just before noon, Anna heard the bell on the front door jangle. "Joyce!" Lupe!" she said, recognizing former colleagues from the hospital. "Have you escaped from the asylum?"

"We're taking an early lunch," Joyce said. "It's the end of the month, and the place is a nuthouse. We had to get out of there."

"You were so smart to quit when you did," Lupe said. "There's talk of more cutbacks."

"Of course, they'll dump us old gals first, so they don't have to pay us our pensions. I've got a year left to go, and Lupe's got eighteen months," Joyce said.

"Our prison sentences."

"They won't fire you," Anna said. "You two are the hospital's institutional memory, the ones who know who's who and what's what and where the bodies are buried."

"Maybe that's the problem," Lupe said. "We do know where the bodies are buried."

"I don't think the new jefes care," Joyce said. "But let's not talk about the office."

"It's sure not the same without you and your jokes and your infectious optimism."

"We miss you, girl. And we're jealous because you had the courage to go out and create your own job. I wish I could do what you did."

"Me, too," said Lupe. "Look at these beautiful glasses, Joyce. See how the light shines through and turns them rainbow colors?"

"You have such gorgeous stuff, Anna. How do you keep from taking it all home?"

"Because I can't eat it. Having your own store has its downside. If you don't sell things, you can't pay your bills, and if you don't pay your bills, you lose your biz. Then you really don't eat."

"Scary," Lupe said. "You've got huevos, chica. Even if I had the money to open a business, I don't think I could deal with the constant worry of making ends meet."

"Me, neither," Joyce said. "Sell us something, and we'll at least help you pay your light bill for the month. Yasmín, the part-time cashier, is getting married on Valentine's Day. The whole office pitched in to buy her a wedding present—from you."

"She'll be thrilled to get a gift from your store," Lupe said.

126

Anna went to an ACLU cocktail party in the spring with Pete, who was on the organization's board. She was sipping a glass of wine and chatting with him when Harry made his way toward her through the crowd. She politely introduced the men to each other. As Anna's longtime confidant, Pete knew all about the weekend at White Cliff Farms and Harry's odd behavior. With a knowing smile, he excused himself and headed for the cash bar.

Harry stood a healthy distance from Anna, watching her over the rim of the drink he was guzzling. "Now will you tell me why you're so ticked off at me? I really do miss you and our evenings together."

To her surprise, Anna didn't need to mentally rehearse her reply. Her words came swiftly and on target. "You were unbelievably rude to me the minute we arrived at White Cliff Farms, and after all our years of what I thought was friendship, it was damn shabby of you."

Harry shoved a large cheese cracker into his mouth and chewed it noisily before swallowing it in a single gulp that made his Adam's apple jump. "Anna, dear, I become totally absorbed when I'm out on the rez," he said, swiping the crumbs from his moustache with a paper napkin. "It's such a deeply spiritual place for me—the sky, the people, the landscape, the vibe. Guess you don't understand that."

Anna set her wine glass down. Slowly and emphatically, she said, "Harry, you are completely full of shit," and walked off.

PART II The Flood

Anna's business prospered. She did better than break even her first year, and in her second year, she was earning almost as much money as she had working at the hospital. "I'll never make a million dollars at this," she told Darcy. "But it's marvelous job, and it suits me."

"I'm pleased to see you doing well, girlfriend," Darcy said. "You've worked so hard to make a go of it."

But early one Sunday morning that summer Anna got a call from Pete.

"Sorry to bother you, doll," he said, "but your store's flooding."

Anna looked out her bedroom window. "How can that be? The sky is cloudless."

"I was loading my luggage into the car a minute ago when I noticed your parking lot is full of water, and it seems to be flowing into your store. I think a drunk driver hit the fire hydrant on the corner last night. Water's still gushing out of it. I called the city, but so far no one has shown up."

"Aw, shit! I can't believe this!"

"Brace yourself, doll, it's gonna be a huge mess. I'd stay and help you clean up, but Ed and I have a plane to catch. We're appraising an antiques collection in San Francisco and won't be back for a couple of days. I'm really, really sorry."

Anna rushed to her store where a battered Chevy truck was perched atop the fire hydrant like a mating dog. Water and mud from the parking lot were swirling into her low-lying adobe. She slogged her way inside, gasping at the cold, dirty water that filled her store almost a foot deep. She was heartsick. All that work. But this was no time for lamentations. She grabbed the baskets floating past and flung them out the side door into a patio that was higher than the floodwaters. Working as fast as she could, she whisked textiles from lower shelves and threw them outside in soggy heaps. She dragged out waterlogged display cubes, furniture, rugs, and boxes of files, setting them to dry on benches in the sun.

A man from the Albuquerque Water Department finally showed up an hour later to turn off the hydrant, but water continued to drain into her building from the parking lot. She paused to catch her breath. A long, low, involuntary moan escaped her as she surveyed the damage. "Christ!" she swore. Her cheerful, tidy store was now a wretched disaster scene. At least a third of her merchandise was seriously damaged. Many new and vintage textiles, pillows, rugs, books on design, and paper goods she'd bought with her scarce capital were not salvageable. The effort she and her friends had put into converting the run-down building into a chic little shop had dissolved in the deluge. Along with her savings. Especially with a mortgage and a business loan hanging over her head, she couldn't afford to be closed even for a few days. Of course, she did carry insurance . . .

A deep, masculine voice interrupted her glum recitative. "Anyone need a lifeguard in there? I'm certified."

A tall Native American with a huge video camera on his shoulder filled the doorway. Behind him, a heavily made-up woman with a big pouffy hairdo was dancing up and down in stocking feet in the turbid water, holding a pair of delicate leather spike heels in her hand and shrieking. Anna recognized her as a weekend TV anchor, Brianna something.

"Fulton!" Brianna screeched to the cameraman. "I am NOT going in there. They don't pay me enough to risk my neck like that. Fuck! Who knows what's floating around in that shit. My shoes are already ruined. And it stinks. Pee yuu."

"Hang on, Brianna," he said patiently. "Two seconds of film—that's all I need. Jesus," he said, looking around the flooded store. He noticed a sweaty and mud splattered Anna standing still in water halfway to her knees, her eyes blank as a stuffed deer's. "Are you OK, ma'am?"

"Of course not," Anna said as tears ran down her face.

"I'm really sorry. Jeez, what a mess. Maybe some footage would help you with your insurance claim. You do have insurance, don't you?"

Anna nodded, blowing her nose on one of the few remaining dry cloth napkins in her inventory.

"Do you feel up to a quick interview?"

She shrugged. "I guess it could be helpful to have a video of what the place looks like now that Noah has left for higher ground."

Just then, Brianna let out an ear-piercing scream. "Eeee, a fucking rat! It's coming straight at me!" She wheeled around, and prancing through the mucky parking lot, fled toward the TV news van parked at the curb.

Anna calmly watched the rat swishing its body through

her flooded showroom. "This guy's an excellent swimmer," she said. "Look at that. He uses his tail for a rudder, like a beaver."

Fulton whooped with laughter, then filmed the oversized rodent as it swam past him and disappeared out the door. After the interview, he set his camera down on the desk. "You did remarkably well. I don't think I could have been as articulate under the circumstances.

"I thought I was a blubbering idiot."

"No, you were terrific and amazingly calm. Look, I have to get back to the station, but I can lend you a hand for a minute or two. That ditz—excuse me, Brianna—needs to chill for a bit. How can I help?"

"You look pretty strong. Would you mind moving things—like maybe those art books?" she asked him. "They're probably kinda heavy now that they're waterlogged. I'd be happy to pay you . . ."

"Don't be silly," he said, manhandling an armload of wet books out the side door to the patio. After a few trips, he excused himself. "Sorry, I can't stay longer. I have to get the footage back to the station for the evening news. Here's my card. I'll check in with you later. What's your phone number?"

Anna realized she needed more help and fast. She called her cousin Sally, who lived ten blocks from the store in the upscale Country Club neighborhood.

"Darling, I'd love to help," Sally said. "But I'm busy cleaning house myself with Esmeralda. We're getting ready for the caterers. The entire symphony board is coming for a dinner party Thursday evening, and my house is a shambles. Maybe I could stop by next weekend to see how you're doing?"

After Anna hung up, she groused at herself for calling Sally. "She's cleaning house with her maid on a Sunday? I doubt it. Oh—a flood? How inconvenient. She's the last person who'd pitch in. She might chip her nail polish."

"Hey, Anna! You in there?" a voice interrupted. Darcy, her six-month-old baby boy riding her hip, stood in the doorway, taking stock of the disheveled store, the bean soup colored floodwaters, the dripping rugs hung over empty racks, and a dirt daubed, bedraggled, and frazzled Anna. "I was driving past and saw the flood. Jesus Christ, what happened?"

Anna sobbed.

Darcy never asked if Anna needed help. She set the baby in his car seat on the desk and gave him a ring of plastic keys and a cracker. Then she fetched a hose from the side yard and began spraying the muddy water out the back door.

Anna yelped. "What are you doing? The last thing we need in here is more water."

Darcy laughed. "You fight water with water," she said brightly. "We've got to get the muck up off the floor before it dries and turns into cement."

"How do you know to do this?"

"I grew up on a farm in Missouri, where floods were part of the landscape."

Darcy made jokes as they worked alongside each other,

helping take Anna's mind off the disaster. The irony of her friend's coming to her aid was not lost on Anna. Darcy had ample excuses for not helping. She and her mother had recently moved her father to an Alzheimer's care facility, and her mother was deeply upset. Darcy's husband, Joe, and their toddler daughter were home with the flu.

They got most of the goop off the floors within a couple of hours, sweeping the water out the back door. There was still a lot of work to do, but Anna insisted Darcy go home. The baby had begun to fuss.

"I'll try to find cleaning help for tomorrow," she said. "Before I hung up on my cousin, she suggested I hire one of those cleaning services, the Merry Maids or something way too cheerful like that. I'll bet they charge a fortune."

"Call Dial-A-Teen," Darcy suggested. "The kids work hard, they really need the money, and even minimum wage is OK with them."

Anna spent the rest of Sunday doing what she could to save her damaged inventory and store fixtures, and to clean the dirt brown residue off the walls and furniture. By the time she got home, she was exhausted, filthy, and demoralized. "How am I going to pay my bills?" she muttered to herself as she showered and got ready to collapse into bed. "Am I going to lose the business I worked so hard to build? Am I going to have to go back to work at that awful hospital?"

Early the next morning, she called Dial-A-Teen.

"We'll send a helper as soon as possible," a young woman said.

Then Anna called her insurance agent.

"Oh, sorry you've had a problem, dear. A Travelers claims adjuster will be there soon. Maybe she could even come today."

Sophie, the girl who came from Dial-A-Teen, showed up half an hour later. She lived only a few blocks away and was free to work all day. She was bright and pleasant. Without Anna's telling her what to do, she grabbed a mop and filled a pail with soapy water.

Anna watched Sophie briskly swab the floors. "How come you're so talented with a mop?" she asked.

"My sibs and I help out in our parents' restaurant, and I'm the mopster," Sophie said. "There's ten of us kids. My dad's Italian and Hispano, and my mom's Pueblo Indian, from San Felipe. I'll be a senior at Albuquerque High."

"What's next after high school?"

"I'm saving money to go to college to study nursing."

"Good for you," Anna said. "I can tell you're a take-charge kind of gal and a hard worker. You'll make a wonderful nurse."

Sophie grinned shyly as she swished the mop across the wooden floorboards.

The claims adjuster, a pinched face woman in high heels, arrived that afternoon. Her beige sweater and skirt were wrapped tightly around her bulging frame like Ace bandages.

Anna stood by nervously as the woman glanced into each of the store's three rooms. "I feel awful," she said mostly to herself, her arms clutching her waist. "My dream store's a muddy wreck. My inventory is ruined. It stinks in here of rot and mold and dead things. This place was knee deep in putrid water yesterday, and a lot of it has simply sunk into the ground under the floorboards."

Anna knew she was babbling, and the claims adjustor was ignoring her, but she couldn't stop herself from thinking aloud. "It could be months before my place dries out completely. Worse, what if the ground squirrels that live under the building drowned in the flood? There was even a rat. Did you see the coverage on last night's news?"

The claims adjustor shrugged. "Frankly, honey, I don't see much damage," she said, scribbling something on her clipboard. "You'll be back on your feet right away. I doubt you're going to lose any business." Suddenly she sneezed repeatedly. "Sorry, I have to leave now. I'm highly allergic to mold."

Anna followed her into the parking lot. "Excuse me, but if you can't stay in there because of the stench, do you think my customers will? They're going to have the same reaction you did. In fact, four different groups of people have already come in this morning. They left immediately, because they said it smells like something died in there. Of course I'm losing business!"

The woman abruptly turned away, and still sneezing, got into her gleaming late model Lexus and drove off in a hurry, her tires spitting mud on the store windows Sophie had just cleaned.

Anna was furious. "I have faithfully paid her company's outrageous insurance premiums since I opened this store, I've had my house and car insurance with Travelers forever, I've never filed an insurance claim in my life, and this is how they treat me when I obviously have a significant loss?" she ranted to Sophie. "I'm going to Thrift Town, and I'm going to buy a cheap umbrella. That's the Travelers Insurance Company's logo. I'm going to cut a million holes in it and send it to the chairman of the board with a note saying if they're truthful about their coverage, this is the umbrella they should be using in their ads."

Sophie giggled. She thought Anna was blowing off steam. But Anna meant it, and she did it.

That night, Pete called from San Francisco to see how she was doing.

"It looks like I'm not going to get a dime from the insurance company," she wailed. "They're basically telling me to jump in the lake."

"Darlin,' anyone who walks into your store is jumping into a lake."

"This isn't funny."

"I know it's not, doll. It's awful. I'm sorry if I sounded flippant. I'm trying to make you feel better."

Anna continued her tirade. "You should have seen that fat, smug bitch. 'I don't see much damage, honey,'" she prattled like a bratty teenager. "What a total dragon lady. And I'm not her fucking honey."

"Claims adjustors have to be able to breathe fire, though their hearts are made of ice. That's the job description."

"I'm not making any sales because of the condition of the building and the parking lot, and I've got to get money quickly if I'm going to make my mortgage and bank-loan payments. What am I going to do?"

Pete knew Anna was rattled and probably a little desperate. "I've got an idea," he said. "Do you still have that gorgeous Tiffany lamp your grandmother left you?"

"Yeah . . ."

"Ed still talks about it, and he hasn't seen it in at least five years. If you're up for selling it, he'll take it off your hands in a heartbeat. For major bucks. The people he did the appraisal for here in The City paid him in cash so he's flush for a change."

"Really? I mean, I love that lamp, but it's way too formal for me. It doesn't fit in my house or the store, and I'm always terrified it'll get knocked over. Would Ed still be interested in it?"

"Anna, he'd kill for it. That is, if you're ready to part with it."

"I've been saving it for a rainy day," she said.

"No rain, doll, but way too much water," Pete said. "Let me talk with him, and I'll call you back."

Anna made up her mind to sell the lamp to Ed or anyone else who'd give her what it was worth. "I adore that thing," she thought wistfully. "I've always loved the way the glass shade gleams like rubies, emeralds and amethysts when you switch it on. But Grandmother Lilly would understand. She was a practical woman."

Ed called her himself, his voice brimming with excitement. They set up an appointment to meet day after next in Santa Fe at his antiques shop. If Anna couldn't get someone to mind her store, she'd simply put a closed sign on the door.

Sophie reappeared exactly on time at 8 a.m. the next morning. They chatted as she and Anna continued to clean.

"I know how we run my family's restaurant, but how does a store work? Is it OK for me to ask?"

"Of course. It's pretty simple. Basically, retail's theater. You're on stage, and the customers are your audience. They come in; you greet them pleasantly; you give them general information about the things you have; you're not too pushy; you don't follow them around—unless you get a bad vibe from them. Then you really follow them."

"Do you get a lot of shoplifters?"

"No. I'd guess it's hard to fence placemats and paper flowers for any kind of serious money. Thieves are after pricey things they can sell easily to buy drugs or booze. Most customers are honest. Knock on wood. So far, nobody's given me a bad check."

"So how do you make a sale?"

"If you see they're interested in something, a handwoven textile, for example, you offer a little information, like where it's made, out of what materials. You suggest how the customer might use it—as a table runner, across the back of a sofa, on her baby grand piano."

Sophie nodded.

Anna decided to take a risk. Although the girl was only sixteen, she was quick and personable, and seemed completely trustworthy. "Would you be willing to handle the store tomorrow while I go to Santa Fe?" she asked.

"I'd be happy to, but I've never worked in a shop," Sophie said. "I've run the register at my parents' restaurant, though."

"I'm sure you can manage. I don't have a cash register. In fact, I keep the change in soufflé cups in the desk drawer. I'll open up for you in the morning, then be back before closing. Chances are, not many people will come by, especially since the parking lot is still a gooey mudhole. If there's a possibility of making a few sales while you're cleaning anyway, it'd be a big help to me."

"OK," Sophie said. "I guess I can try."

"You'll be perfect," Anna said.

A friend of Anna's came by to pick up a pair of pillows she had on layaway. Fortunately, they'd been stored on the upper shelf of a closet with other layaways and were undamaged.

At Anna's direction, Sophie wrote up the sale without a hitch. "This kid's a godsend," she thought.

Anna was putting down a layer of wax on the floor of the main room when she heard a knock at the door. "Anna, you still alive?" a deep voice rang out.

She put down her sponge mop and went to investigate.

The TV cameraman leaned against the doorframe. "Hi, I'm Fulton. Remember me? Here I am. Ready to do your bidding," he said with a wide grin. He looked around the store. "Wow, you've made a lot of progress. I'm impressed."

Anna sighed deeply. "It's still a mess. Maybe I should throw in the towel. Maybe I wasn't meant to be a shopkeeper."

"C'mon. Giving up is not an option. When disaster strikes, you throw down the gauntlet and pick up the towel. You don't strike me as a quitter."

"I'm not," Anna said. "But the insurance company blew me off. They said I won't miss out on any sales, and they won't give me anything for my wrecked store or my soggy inventory. Of course I'm losing business. How am I ever going to keep it going?" Anna began to whimper and then stopped herself.

"Sorry about the self-pity."

"Not to worry. It's understandable. Now, how can I be useful?"

Anna thought for a minute. "Could you possibly help me move the furniture back in from the patio?" she asked tentatively. "That's something I can't do by myself."

They picked up chairs, bookcases, and shelves, and arranged them in the main room.

Once they'd put things in order, Fulton stood up, leaned backward, and cracked his spine. "Now I hope you're not one of those women who wants to rearrange the furniture ten times before she's happy with the way it looks."

"Of course not," Anna said. "Um . . . but don't you think that chair would be better in this corner?"

"I knew it!" Fulton said. "Actually, it would look better over there, though I kind of hate to admit it."

After they moved the chair, Anna surveyed the room. "It almost looks like my store again."

"Where's the furniture oil?" Fulton said. "I love polishing wood."

———————

Anna called Darcy the minute Fulton left. "You won't believe this, but the cameraman came back."

"To shoot more footage?"

"No. He came to help me. We moved the furniture back inside, and he polished all the wood like he was enjoying himself. Then we had red enchiladas at Duran's Pharmacy. He's fabulous."

"I remember you told me he was a handsome guy."

"That he is. But he's also an exceptional person. He made me laugh, he did a lot of heavy lifting, he paid for dinner—Harry always insisted we go Dutch—and he loves Zydeco. We're going to the Queen Ida concert next weekend. He's exactly three months younger than me, and he's an English major from Dartmouth."

"Oh, baby!" Darcy said. "An English major. Be still my beating heart. Enough of those decrepit doctor types, girlfriend."

Anna returned from Santa Fe the following afternoon wearing a big smile. Ed told her the lamp was worth much more than she'd thought. He wrote her a hefty check for it on the spot. She was in the clear for at least a few months.

"I had a great day, too," Sophie said proudly. "I put down two coats of wax in the back rooms AND I made three hundred dollars. A friend of yours saw the flood on TV and bought two sets of those Italian glasses, a couple of embroidered tablecloths, and matching napkins. I hope you don't mind, but I gave her a box of the water-damaged books for five dollars. She said she was going to cut them up for collage."

"What a wonderful idea. Five dollars certainly beats the zero the insurance company will give me for them. If you decide not to go to nursing school, I'm sure you can get a job in retail. You've certainly got the correct instincts."

Anna gave Sophie a big hug. "I don't know what I would've done without you. If I survive this setback, it'll be due in no small measure to your wonderful help."

Sophie glowed.

"I wish I could offer you a part-time job today, but I know school's starting soon. Would you be willing to help me out from time to time?"

"Sure," Sophie said. "This is fun. It's like playing store when I was a kid."

"Can you come this Friday afternoon?"

"I'm sorry, I can't. I'm leaving town tomorrow for maybe six weeks. My Aunt Bernarda out in Gallup fell and broke her leg yesterday, and my mom's sending me to help her with her errands and gardening. My uncle's in Canada for the rest of the summer. He's a medicine man."

A flashbulb went off in Anna's head. "Is your aunt by any chance Bernarda Tom?"

Sophie stared at her. "Yes. Do you know her?"

"I do! A couple of years ago, I met her out on the Navajo reservation. Your uncle did a ceremonial for a group of medical students I was with. I helped your aunt harvest her corn crop, and she gave me some beautiful multicolored ears. I plant seeds from them every spring. San Felipe corn. I always remember Bernarda when I'm tending my garden."

Sophie tipped her head at Anna. "You're the one who found the arrowhead," she said. "My uncle told us that story."

Anna laughed. "Yeah, I think he was testing us. You know how grabby Anglos are about artifacts and potshards. He put that arrowhead at the base of the rain barrel outside the sweat lodge where one of us was bound to find it."

"No, he didn't. He told my family one of the women found it, the doc's friend, the one who wasn't a medical student. Was that you?"

"Yeah," Anna said.

"My uncle was really touched because you gave him the arrowhead. I've seen it. It's beautiful, a very special gift. He says he treasures it and keeps it in his medicine bundle."

"Wow," Anna said. "How about that."

Anna drove home in a bit of a daze. The fact that Sophie and Dan Tom were related was almost too much for her. She called Darcy. "What do you make of it?"

"It's a coincidence, girlfriend. They do happen, you know. That's why there's such a word."

"You're no help," Anna said.

"What? You want me to say it's cosmic? OK, it's cosmic. I thought you hated New Age everything."

"I do," Anna said. "New Age rhymes with sewage."

On a fall afternoon a couple of years later, Anna closed the store early and drove to the airport to pick up Fulton. She immediately spotted him coming up the ramp from the passenger gates into the terminal. He was a head taller than most of the other passengers and had a unique, lumbering walk she could spot a mile away. When he spied her, he rushed past the startled security guard. Grinning, he threw his arms around her, picked her up, and spun her, her pink tiered skirt whirling and enveloping them both like a hibiscus flower in motion.

He set her down again, and holding hands, they walked toward the escalators that led to the baggage claim area.

"How was New Hampshire?"

"Green," said Fulton. "I forget how green everything is there. Hey, speaking of green, can we stop at Garcia's on the way home for a green chile burrito? After a week back East, I'm suffering from serious chile withdrawal."

Anna and Fulton sat on the front porch swing of the little house in Duranes they'd shared for the past year and discussed their week.

"You first," Fulton said. "How's the store?"

"Business has been flourishing. Plus I found a supplier for Tarahumara baskets and dolls. They're a husband and wife team of anthropologists, and their prices are so reasonable, I'll bet they don't make a dime. Tell me about your trip."

Fulton had spent the week at a conference at Dartmouth as a consultant on Native American student issues. "Things have really changed, I'm happy to report. For the most part, it's easier for Native kids than when I went there in the '80s when it was still mostly white males from privileged families. Those guys' points of reference were the stock market, the golf course, sailing, sports cars, and debutantes. Now the student body is much more mixed. Girls! Black kids! Asians! Latinos! Natives from every part of North America! These students are much better prepared than I was. They've traveled, they're Internet savvy, and they're proud of their heritage, not ashamed of it."

"I can't believe you were ever less than proud of being Navajo, " Anna said.

"At the very least, I knew the skills my community valued—helping my grandma with her sheep, knowing how to field dress an elk, understanding the basics of a Blessing Way ceremony—were completely alien to mainstream American culture. Boy, was I a fish outta water, coming from the rez. Today the school's intent on retaining Native kids, helping them when they're overwhelmed by missing home. I was really homesick this trip myself. It was an exceptionally long week without you." Fulton hugged her close and kissed her.

"I'm thrilled to have you home. I missed you, too."

They drove west to visit Fulton's family in Teec Nos Pos in October. Golden cottonwoods outlined the arroyos, creeks, and valleys beneath the cloudless skies of western New Mexico. The weather was neither too hot nor too cold; the tourists and their RVs were mostly gone.

On the way, they passed the turnoff to White Cliff Farms. Anna hadn't thought about her weekend there for a long time. She retold the story, this time with details she hadn't told Fulton before, like how Harry's bizarre behavior and

Bernarda's revelations about his philandering had shocked her. They reminisced about the Great Flood, where they'd met so romantically watching a swimming rat. That sent them into peals of laughter.

"It was such an astonishing coincidence that it was Sophie who showed up to help me out," Anna said. "I still can't believe it."

Fulton nodded thoughtfully. "It doesn't surprise me in the least that someone from Dan Tom's family was the one to bail you out of the flood."

"Really? Think of it, though. What are the chances of her being the one kid Dial-A-Teen sends over, in a city of half a million people?"

"Ah, you're thinking like an Anglo."

"Of course. I am an Anglo. Mostly, anyway. It's part of my DNA to demand rationality."

"Not everything that happens is rational, as far as I can tell," he said.

"I mean, Sophie coming to help me out is like an O. Henry story, where at the end, everything fits together neatly like a puzzle."

"Isn't life a puzzle?"

"Yeah, but it's rare to have all the pieces."

"True. Yet once in a while, things do work out in a tidy fashion. One of my aunties used to say: 'God works his wonders in mischievious ways.' You gave a beautiful gift to Dan Tom, so when you really needed help, he—or part of his family—gave *you* a beautiful gift."

"Hmmm," Anna said. She mused on that for a few more miles. "I guess that's true. I mean, it certainly seems things work out like that, at least sometimes. I've always thought people communicate with each other in ways we don't yet understand. You know, you'll suddenly think of a person you haven't thought about in years, and then the telephone rings and it's them. It's mental telephony!"

"Yup," Fulton said. "It's happened to me more than once. I also think events can be connected like links in a circular chain. It all comes back to you, the good as well as the bad."

As they traversed the dramatic, nearly treeless landscape of the Navajo reservation, Anna's eyes explored the vermilion earth and the craggy, red stone skyscrapers that pointed their spires toward a flawless, blue cabochon sky. The hawks sitting on telephone wires. The abandoned hogans. The dirt roads that seemed to lead off to nowhere. The hundred car long trains traversing the far off horizon, their multiple diesel engines trailing plumes of black smoke.

"Whatever happened to Sophie?" Fulton asked.

"She never did come back to work for me. She found herself a boyfriend out in Gallup and stayed there with Bernarda for her last year of high school. I don't know if she went to nursing school, but I hope she did. She was a straight-A student."

"And how's Harry?" Fulton asked with a wry grin. "The old rat himself."

"I never saw him again after that ACLU party, but funny you should ask. The other day, Darcy told me she'd seen a man coming out of the Flying Star on Central, holding hands with Harry's ex-wife, Irene. He looked feeble—white haired and hunched over. Maybe he was a little senile. Darcy said his head bobbled the way her dad's did from Alzheimer's. She thought it was Harry."

After a few minutes of pensive silence, Fulton said: "I have a question."

"Shoot," Anna replied.

With one eye on the road ahead and the other on Anna, he smiled the subtle little smile that so endeared him to her, and asked: "Did the chairman of the board of the Travelers Insurance Company ever acknowledge getting the umbrella you sent him?"

Anna laughed. "I never heard from him. But I follow their stock, and they haven't done so well lately."

Fulton got a good laugh out of that.

6

GUAPO

Looking for the source of a faint animal whimper, Rosalía Martínez knelt in the gravel and peered into the shadows under the truck next to hers. A bloody, badly mauled dog growled and snapped at her. She stood up, took a deep breath, and wiped her dusty palms on her Levis. "Damn!" she said as she strode purposefully through the row of parked vehicles to the main door of the Del Valle Vet Clinic. Sticking her head inside, she called to one of her vet techs.

"Veronica? Can you give me a hand out front for a minute? And bring a package of hot dogs, will you?"

"Are you having a sudden attack of the munchies, jefa?"

"No, we have a hurt dog out here under Josie's pickup. I'm going to need help getting him out of there."

Veronica, a package of franks in hand, quickly arrived on the scene. She bent down and looked under the truck. The dog bared its teeth at her with a menacing snarl, warning her off. "This could take awhile, you know," she said as she straightened up.

Rosalía signed. "I thought yesterday was a tough day, pulling two calves out of two mama cows thirty miles apart. At least it's the middle of the week and business is slow."

For half an hour, the women worked patiently to coax the dog out from under the truck. Rosalía tossed him a hot dog. He snatched it hungrily, wolfing it down in a couple of bites. She threw another one under the truck, and another, each time closer to daylight. Groaning with pain, the dog dragged himself forward, each agonizing move bringing him further toward the food. Rosalía lured him out inch by inch. She could see he was starving. His ribs and hipbones showed through his filthy coat. His ears were ripped, his scabrous fur crawled with ticks and fleas, and saliva ran from the side of his torn mouth. When she'd enticed him more than halfway out and his teeth were firmly clamped on a wiener, she grabbed him by the scruff of the neck and held him while Veronica jabbed a tranquilizer into his rump. He slumped into submission. Veronica fetched a flea spray. They doused him with insecticide before they carried him into the clinic and laid him out on an examining table.

"Boy howdy, as they say in Texas. Where've ya been, buster?" Rosalía said to the unconscious dog.

"Are you really going to try to save him? He's a mess."

"Yep. Rosalía Martínez, Fool with a capital F. Who needs another homeless mutt? But look at this fellow. Underneath all the crud, he's a blue heeler. A cow dog. A working dog. Something tells me he's worth the effort."

"OK," Veronica said skeptically. "You're the boss. Where do we start?"

"First, let's clean him up. He looks like he's been in a helluva fight. Maybe he was being used for bait."

"Bait?"

Rosalía nodded. "Sheriff Velásquez tells me somebody in the county is stealing dogs and picking up strays, feeding them to their pit bulls—practice for dog fights."

"Ugh. People really do things like that?"

"Not real people—more like sadistic scumbags who get off on being cruel to animals. Let me know when you've got him as clean as possible. Meanwhile, I'll tend to our clients."

The stray dog's survival was in doubt for several days. He had lost a lot of blood, his hind leg was broken in two places, he had a nasty head wound, an infected eye, an enlarged spleen, and a list of other injuries. Out of his good eye, he regarded the women caring for him with a look they could only interpret as gratitude. Once it appeared he was going to make it, Rosalía named him Guapo.

"Handsome?" Veronica laughed. "He is anything but."

"Hey, show a little appreciation. Look at the handsome suturing job I did on him."

"Yeah, but he's never going to look like anything but a scarred-up mutt."

"Shhhhh! You're going to give him a complex."

Rosalía and her crew took advantage of a mild, sunny afternoon to eat lunch at the picnic table under the apricot tree behind the clinic. A much improved Guapo limped around the table, cadging bites. As each one turned him down, he sighed in disappointment and then tottered on to the next potential sucker. He stopped beside Veronica.

"No people food for you, dude," she said. He cocked his head at her and looked so pitiful that she tossed him a tidbit of ham from her sandwich.

"What are we going to do with this pooch?" Rosalía wondered aloud. "He's almost healthy enough now to get a new home."

As if Guapo knew she was talking about him, he hobbled over to her, rested his chin on her thigh, and looked up at her with large, liquid eyes. "No, mi amor," she groaned. "I am not taking you home with me. My roommate and I agreed: no more critters. We already have a dog, two horses, a goat, and three cats."

"Speaking of cats," Josie said. "Mrs. Rael's prissy Persian took one look at Guapo the other day and tried to climb the Venetian blinds."

"Wish I'd seen that," Veronica said. "That damn cat bites me every time he comes in here."

"With his leg cast, torn ears, stitches, and bandages, Guapo looks a little scary to our human clientele, too," Josie added. "Mrs. Rodríguez is terrified of him, and so are some of the little kids."

"That settles it," Rosalía said to Guapo. "Sorry, amigo. You're forever banished from the waiting room. Can't have you running off the paying customers."

Guapo stayed at the clinic for the time being and became the official staff pet. One morning, he sat beside Veronica, watching her put the finishing touches on a toy poodle's trim. She started to sing a bouncy New Mexican nonsense song called "Frijolitos Pintos":

Frijolitos pintos, claveles morados,
Ay como sufren los enamorados.

Guapo raised his muzzle and warbled a tune that seemed to mimic her voice. Veronica stopped. "Oh, my God. You sing!" She sang louder. The dog bayed his version of her tune:

Mamacita Linda, ahí viene Vicente.
Sácale un banquito pa' que se siente.

Laughing, she put down her clippers and called the rest of the staff. "Hey, Josie! Ramón! Come here a second." They gathered around the perplexed poodle as Veronica sang:

Le dió la viruela, le dió el sarampión.
Le quedó la cara como un chicharrón.

Guapo yowled on, confident as a Pavarotti, his voice wavering in something approaching a melody. Josie and Ramón joined in, singing more of the song, clapping in time to the music, with Guapo in the spotlight as if he were the lead tenor performing his signature aria.

Ahí viene mi suegra bajando la loma,
Brinca la leña, y echa la maroma.

Rosalía walked in looking stern. "What on earth is going on? We've got people out there waiting."

"OK, we're fired. But first, get a load of this, jefa," Veronica said. She and her coworkers began to intone the song's last verse. Guapo craned his neck back and yipped along with them.

Una perra pinta, pinta y orejona,
Se busca la cola y la tiene rabona.

Rosalía laughed till she cried. "This is hilarious. I knew that dog was worth saving."

"We can go on Letterman with him," Veronica said.

In the clinic's barn on a quiet afternoon, Guapo lay napping in the hay while Rosalía changed the bandage on a horse's leg where it had cut itself on barbed wire. The moment a cowboy stepped in to check on his horse, the dog jumped to his feet. Dragging his leg cast, he excitedly trotted toward the man, wagging his tail effusively. The cowboy reached down and patted Guapo's scarred head.

"Hey, buddy, looks like you been in a barroom brawl. Damn—what's the other guy look like?"

Guapo sniffed the cowboy's outstretched hand, then his tail drooped. He returned to Rosalía and lay down at her feet. Again and again, she saw him approach other cowboys in the same hopeful way, but each time he was disappointed.

"You must have been some rancher's pal, eh, Guapo?" she said.

During the Del Valle Vet's monthly spay and neuter clinic, a handsome cowboy with a shiny, black handlebar moustache stopped at the receptionist's desk. He set down a carrier with a large orange cat in it, removed his tall hat, and smoothed his thick, black hair back from his forehead. "I'm here to drop off my mother's cat," he announced.

"Do you have an appointment?" Josie asked.

"Yep, Name's García. Well, not the cat. I'm García—he's Bozo. Don't get us mixed up, now. He's supposed to get fixed, and I'm not quite ready for that."

Rosalía looked up from her computer. "You're sure?" she teased. "We have a special on this week—two for the price of one."

"I'm very sure, ma'am," the cowboy said with a wide grin.

Although Guapo had been blackballed from the waiting room, he appeared out of nowhere, trotted up to the cowboy, sat at his feet, and energetically thumped his tail on the floor. The man hunkered down on the heels of his polished boots, put his hand under the dog's jaw, and spoke softly: "Look at you, you old cow dog. I bet you've got quite a story to tell."

Suddenly, Rosalía had an inspiration. "Mr. García," she said with her most fetching smile, "you need that dog."

The cowboy studied her and tugged at the ends of his drooping moustache. "Ma'am?"

"I'm gonna guess you're a real rancher, and a real rancher needs a real cow dog—like this guy. He's had all his shots, and he comes with a free fifty-pound bag of dog chow, a collar, and tags."

"Actually, I am a real rancher. You're right about that. And truth is, my old Nessie is too arthritic to keep up with the cows anymore. But what makes you think I need this particular dog?"

"You need that dog because he will make you smile."

"He will? I sure could use a few smiles."

Rosalía cleared her throat and, to his astonishment, she began to sing in a lyrical voice: "Oh, give me a home, where the buffalo roam . . ."

As if on cue, Guapo threw his head back, and howled and wailed and yodeled along with her song. Everyone in the reception area burst out laughing.

The cowboy roared, slapping his hat against the thigh of his faded jeans. "Dang! That dog sings. No kidding, he does make me smile. Excuse me for saying so, but you've got a beautiful smile yourself, as a matter of fact. By any chance does that dog come with a pretty vet to take care of him?"

Guapo went home with the cowboy, Abelardo—Abe—García. A week later, Abe called Rosalía. "You do make house calls, don't you?" he asked.

"Guapo's not doing well?" Rosalía was concerned.

"Oh, he's thriving. He comes in real handy. In fact, he's the perfect excuse for me to invite you out to my ranch this weekend. To check up on your patient, of course. And have lunch with us."

Rosalía wasn't sure who the "us" was, but she decided to accept the invitation. A drive in the country that did not involve work was a welcome break from her long days at the clinic.

Abe's tidy farmstead was perched on a hillside overlooking the Coyote Valley. When she pulled her truck to a stop, she saw Guapo gimping around on his leg cast, happily trying to herd an old barn cat that easily managed to stay out of his reach. Abe had laid out a picnic on a table outside his old-fashioned, tin roofed adobe.

"I hope you like pesto," he said, placing a bowl of warm, green-flecked pasta in front of her. "I made it myself, with piñón nuts from here on the ranch. My lab partner grows basil year round in his greenhouse and shares it with us. It's a job perk."

"I take it you're not a full-time rancher," Rosalía said, heaping her plate with fettuccine, green salad, and fresh fruit.

Abe smiled. "Nope. Behind my aw-shucks and denim facade lies an 'edumacated' type. I'm an industrial hygienist at Los Alamos."

"Eek. A nerd."

"A part-time nerd."

"Promise me you're not making bombs," she said.

"Promise. Unlike some of my colleagues at the lab, we're actually doing something other than finding new, more efficient ways to kill people."

"I'm not exactly sure what an industrial hygienist does."

"That makes two of us. Let me tell you about a project I'm working on, though. It's nifty. We're developing a process that uses carbon dioxide to etch computer chips, so the semiconductor industry can quit contaminating the earth with the acids, solvents, and hazardous air pollutants they use now."

"I thought chip manufacturing was a clean industry."

"Most everybody does, and that's what they want you to

think. Fact is, though, they're terrible polluters, and they are arrogant about it. They don't care that their emissions are toxic to people and animals or that they're trashing the environment. Our new process will cut 90 percent of their water use—which is huge—and eliminate most of the chemicals they need."

"Fascinating. So what did you study in school to become a hygienist?"

"What do you think? Girls, football, basketball, girls ... and now and then, apart from girls, a little chemistry and physics. Finally, I got a master's in environmental science from UNM."

Rosalía bit into a cherry tomato. The setting—the shade of a tall pear tree on a sunny, early fall afternoon—was idyllic. The food was delicious. And the cowboy/scientist was becoming more and more intriguing by the minute.

"My turn for asking questions," Abe said, looking directly into her eyes that were nearly the same shade of deep blue as his own. "How did a lovely lady like you end up in the vet biz, sticking your arms up cows' butts and all?"

Rosalía scowled. "You sound exactly like my uncle."

"Hey, no misogynistic insults intended."

"I was helping Doc out in his clinic by the time I was ten. Mostly I did glamorous tasks like mop cat pee off the floor. Gradually, he let me do more interesting things, like wash and clip dogs. Even though it wasn't kosher, I started giving shots and watching operations. Eventually, he let me suture incisions."

"Um, excuse me for interrupting, but is this uncle you're talking about Doc Alire by any chance?"

"El mismo. He still grouses about how vet work is 'no job for a woman.' I never wanted to be anything else. I got my DVM in Fort Collins, and he sold me the practice when he retired. Pretty much in spite of himself, I think."

"I'm impressed. I've known Doc Alire my whole life. He's been the best vet in the Española Valley forever. If that crotchety old geezer let you take over his practice, you must know what you're doing."

"I get by," Rosalía shrugged shyly.

"I have an idea. If you've finished pretending you like my cooking, let's saddle up a couple of nags and go for a ride around the place. You do ride, don't you?"

"Cowboy, I've been riding horses since you were making mud pies. In fact, I was a champeen barrel racer in my better days."

"Hell, anybody can outrun a barrel."

Rosalía followed Abe into his small tack room, where he gathered up bridles and saddles. She noticed a stamped-silver headstall hanging on the wall.

"That's gorgeous," she said. "Navajo?"

"Yes. My Grandpa Nez made it," Abe said. "He was quite a silversmith until Parkinson's made it impossible for him to keep working. Let me show you the rest." He whisked a blanket off a saddle resting on a sawhorse. Its leather was a deep umber polished by many years of use and saddle soap, its edges trimmed with stamped silver that matched the bridle.

"Wow," Rosalía said. "That's the most beautiful horse gear I've ever seen. The craftsmanship is amazing."

Abe saddled up a tall bay gelding for Rosalía. As he was busy tightening the girth, a brown appaloosa leaned over the corral fence and grabbed Abe's cowboy hat with his teeth.

Abe aimed a friendly swat at the horse and took his hat back. "Ah, Chocolate, up to your old tricks?" The horse nickered and shook his head. "I was going to ride that pinto mare, but I guess Chocolate's telling me he'd like an outing."

"What a good-looking boy you've got there," Rosalía said. "Still a stallion?"

"Yeah. He's fairly mellow for a stud. He's got excellent bloodlines and a wonderful, smooth gait. I'd like to breed him."

They rode uphill on a dirt road that edged neat, lush, green alfalfa fields and pastures, chatting easily like old friends. Abe rode with Guapo lying across the front of his saddle. The autumn air was cool in the shade of the cotton-woods bordering the road but warm in the sun by the creek where they stopped to water the horses and let them graze. Taking Rosalía by the hand, he led her through a maze of currant bushes and Gambel oaks down a hill to his favorite fishing hole. They sat on the flat rocks beside the rivulet, took off their boots, rolled up their pant legs, and dangled their bare feet in the cool water.

"If you sit still enough, you might see some of the wild trout that live in this stream," he said. "I've spent thousands of hours trying to catch those wily little buggers."

"Did you grow up in Coyote?" Rosalía asked.

"Yep. I'm my grandparents' favorite grandchild. Guess

I'd better confess that I'm their only one. They left me this ranch. Grandpa Nez built the house himself."

"Who takes care of things when you're not around?"

"My cousin Sam. He's retired now from the Floresta, the Forest Service. He lives down the road and keeps an eye on my spread."

Rosalía grinned. "So how big is your 'spread,' cowboy?"

"My vast holdings consist of sixteen mother cows, a bull, four horses, thirty acres of irrigated land, about eighty dry acres that are mostly pines and fir. The national forest abuts the property. I graze my cows there in summer."

"Are you here much?"

"I spend weekends and holidays here, if I can. My folks live a few miles away, off Route 96. I need to check up on them more often now that they're getting on. Plus this place helps me be as honest and real as possible. Basically keeps me sane. My wife never liked it, though."

Rosalía's eyebrows rose a notch, but she hoped Abe hadn't noticed.

"She was a city girl, from LA. We met in college back East. She was on scholarship like I was. I think I mistook homesickness for love. I mean, I did love her … "

"You don't have to explain."

"No, but I want to. We got married after graduation and came back to New Mexico, where we could both get state tuition for grad school. She really didn't want to be in the sticks, though. She thrived on big city life. We were OK together, but not terrific. Then she was diagnosed with Hodgkin's lymphoma and went downhill fast. If she hadn't gotten sick, I think we would have split up eventually."

"Abe, I'm so sorry."

"Well, it doesn't matter. She's been gone seven years now."

Rosalía put her arm around his shoulders, and they sat silently looking into the meandering creek for what might have been five minutes or an hour. A few tiny, gold colored trout flashed by and then skittered into a shady spot.

"Have you ever been married?" Abe asked, adding, "I ... I don't mean to pry."

"Oh, I've had some close calls. Let's see—a drunk, a compulsive liar, a depressive, a guy who didn't understand the concept of monogamy ... My mom would see me moping because of this man or that and tell me, "¡Mejor sola que mal acompañada!"

"Your mom gave you first-rate advice. Obviously, being a vet and running your own show, you can stand on your own two feet."

"I wobble a lot, but I can be alone, too."

"What does your mom think about nerds?"

"You'd have to go a long way to find out. After my dad died, she got married again and moved to Bali."

"Bali?" Suddenly, Abe slapped her knee. "Dessert! I almost forgot it. You like tiramisu, dontcha?"

After a few months, Rosalía mostly lived at Abe's "in town" house in Las Colonias, midway between Española and Los Alamos. Her former roommate insisted on keeping all their animals at the place they had shared in Santa Cruz. "Bad enough you're leaving. I'd be too lonely without the critters," she told Rosalía.

Rosalía and Abe were married in the spring. They held hands beneath eighty-year-old apple trees in the orchard behind the Coyote ranch house while Father José conducted the wedding ceremony. Blossoms fluttered in the breeze, falling on the wedding party. Guapo was one of the invited guests. Wearing a starched wing collar and a black bow tie, he sat attentively between Abe and Rosalía, looking from one to the other as they said their vows. At the reception, he entertained the guests, singing along with Conjunto Tapatío's ranchera repertoire.

Abe and Rosalía returned tanned and relaxed from their honeymoon in Playa del Carmen and went directly to the ranch to pick up Guapo. He greeted them effusively, racing around their truck in circles, leaping and pirouetting in the air like a demented ballerina.

"That mutt missed you something terrible," Sam said. "He laid under that crab apple tree the whole time you were gone. Barely ate, barely moved. I thought he might be dying."

Except when Abe was in Los Alamos, Guapo followed him everywhere. He even rode behind Abe's saddle on long treks around the ranch.

"That dog is worse than a love struck teenager," Rosalía said to her husband one morning at breakfast. "He worships the ground you walk on."

"You told me he was smart, Rosie. You weren't wrong, were you?"

"In another seven months, he's going to have to share you with more than just me."

Abe looked up from his huevos rancheros. "Do you mean to tell me . . .?"

"Yep, you're going to be a daddy."

Abe jumped up from the table and threw his arms around her, tears filling his eyes. "I never thought this would happen to me."

"Me neither," she said, simultaneously sniffling and grinning from ear to ear.

Guapo whined and wedged himself between them.

"Your days of being our only child are soon to be history, bud," she said to the dog, who perked up what was left of his ears and tilted his head as if trying to understand her.

Abe called the lab to say he was going to be late.

Rosalía phoned the clinic. "Hi, ladies, it's the jefa. I won't be in today. I'm calling in pregnant."

From across the room, Abe could hear Veronica shriek with delight.

They sat at the kitchen table, holding hands, discussing their future.

"How am I going to manage a baby and the clinic?" Rosalía wondered aloud. "Maybe I should have thought of that before I submitted to your charms."

Abe laughed. "I know a guy who'd give anything to be your house husband. I am so tired of the lab, with its intrigues and political wrangling. Frankly, I don't think it's a healthy place to be, either. I know too much: the leaks, the coverups, the general state of the air and water quality up there. I've been plotting for years to get off the hill and make a living doing something else."

"But what about your supercritical CO_2 project? You've put a lot into that, Abe."

"Yeah, I have. It's technology that could really reduce toxic emissions at places like that Intel plant near Albuquerque. The locals claim the company has been poisoning them for years."

"You're willing to drop the project, just like that?"

"The sad truth is, Rosie, we've been shut out by politics and the power of money. We've missed the opportunity for another six years or so of the industrial cycle. I can't sit around waiting for things to change. I'd rather spend my time doing something positive and tangible."

Rosalía propped her elbows on the breakfast table and framed her face with the palms of her hands. "Like what?"

"Like writing software for small ranchers, teaching them how to use computers. I could simplify things for them, come up with programs anybody can learn, even my blockheaded old man. I'd love a stay-at-home job; I'd love to care for our baby."

"I understand how you feel, but we'd lose your income."

"I can consult now and then with the lab for extra cash. I've also thought about selling this place. We don't need two houses."

"You want to move to the ranch?"

"Well, that is, if you do. I like Las Colonias, but it's not far enough away from Los Alamos for us."

"Sweetheart, although I love Coyote and I'm a country

girl at heart, the ranch house isn't exactly in shape for a baby."

"Not now, but Sam and I and a couple more cousins could fix it up, add another bath, another bedroom, remodel the kitchen before the baby comes. It'd mean a longer commute for you, living up there, but not by much with the new highway."

"You've worked this all out, haven't you, you schemer."

"Yep. Ever since I met you, in fact, and you foisted that worthless fleabag on me."

The baby turned out to be twins, a boy and a girl they named Mateo and Graciela—Mattie and Chela. When Abe's mother, Emma, first saw the babies in the hospital, each a tight bundle lying on either side of a pale, exhausted-looking Rosalía, tears came to her eyes. She turned to her tall, beaming son. "They look exactly like you did when you were born, Abe. All that black hair, those beautiful rosy faces."

"Would you like to hold them?" Rosalía asked her mother-in-law.

"I might never give 'em back."

"Is that a deal?" Rosalía asked. And fell asleep.

When Rosalía and the babies came home from the hospital, Abe showed her the bay window Sam had made out of three sash windows in the living room. He dramatically swept aside the sheet covering it and laughed to see her gasp at the majestic view.

"I thought you'd like to have a Georgia O'Keeffe over the couch," he said, "but I couldn't afford the real thing."

"Oh, sweetheart, this is the real thing," she sighed as they stood watching the light play on Pedernal Mesa, where it stood like a conning tower above a vast ocean of deep green pine forest and red cliffs.

Emma was thrilled to help take care of her grandchildren. The healthy, happy, dark haired, blue eyed babies grew like weeds. They adored their curly headed, laughing grandmother. When they began to speak, they called her "Ama."

Rosalía hired another vet tech and cut back her office hours to four days a week even though the clinic was growing. Her mother-in-law and Abe shared baby tending duties when Rosalía was at work. The commute gave her precious time alone to collect her thoughts. Sometimes she took the twins with her to the clinic—until they could crawl and get into mischief.

Abe seemed content being a full-time father and rancher. He took on the management of three small, neighboring ranches for their absentee owners. He planted and harvested alfalfa, managed herds with Rosalía's help, taught computer classes at the local senior center. He took the twins with him as much as possible. When they were big enough to hang on, he drove an ATV out to change irrigation sprinklers with one kid in front, the other kid behind, and Guapo trotting beside them. Weekends in warm weather, he and Rosalía would ride their horses up the canyon, each parent holding a child in front on the saddle.

They picnicked by the little trout stream that watered their fields below. The toddlers played in the shallows, splashing and giggling, while their parents lay on an army blanket and watched them. Guapo was never far away. If the kids strayed, he snapped playfully at their heels, herding them back to their parents.

The twins were almost three when Rosalía told her husband, "Honey, we're expanding the herd."

Abe looked up from his newspaper. "We are?"

Rosalía gave a little sob of mock sorrow. "Yes, dear. The rabbit died."

Abe leaped out of his chair and grabbed her. In open-mouthed wonder, the twins watched their parents cavort around the living room.

"Mommy, can I have a rabbit?" Chela asked.

"Not until you're older, sweetie."

The child burst into tears.

"Look, Rosie, I know you're feeling financially pressed with another baby on the way," Abe said later, "but I can take on more consulting work at the lab. My former lab partner—remember Mike? The basil guy?—he says the CO_2 project is on the front burner again."

"I know you'll be happy working on it, if only for a day or two a week, but I worry about the commute. It's so long, and we're having an especially snowy winter."

"True, the roads winding up to Los Alamos can be treacherous," he said. "But the Subaru's got four-wheel drive."

"I insist that you stay overnight at a motel in Los Alamos when the weather is bad. I mean it."

"I'll be careful," he promised. "But you know how much I want to get home to you and the chamacos."

One snowy night in late March when Rosalía was nearly five months pregnant, Abe was later than usual. It was past nine o'clock, and she hadn't been able to reach him on his cellphone or at the lab.

"Dammit, Abe," she yelled at the silent phone. "Call me. You know how I worry."

Heavy, wet snowflakes were coming down harder and larger, sticking to the corners of the windows in droopy isosceles triangles. Near eleven o'clock, she saw head-lights coming slowly up the driveway and breathed a sigh of relief.

But the knock at the front door told her it wasn't her husband. She opened the door to find Sheriff Bertie Velásquez standing on the porch, his hat in hand, his head hanging, his mouth in a tight grimace. He caught her as she fell to the floor in a faint.

A truck carrying radioactive waste down the hill from Los Alamos had lost its brakes and slammed into the rear of Abe's car. Both vehicles went over the edge of the highway, tumbling into a deep canyon. Neither man survived.

Rosalía wept nonstop. Her grief immeasurable, she locked herself in the bedroom she and Abe had shared, the bedroom he had built for them. Their wedding pictures on the bureau now looked like someone else's. His clothes, his boots, even his pocket change were poignant remnants of a man she'd never see again—her funny, generous, thoughtful, brilliant, creative Abe. A wonderful father to their children. The one person in the world she could lean on. The one person she needed most to help her out of this bottomless sorrow.

She finally tired of feeling sorry for herself and summoned the courage to leave her sanctuary. She temporarily turned over management of the clinic to Veronica and stayed home to be with her children. They went for walks in the snow. They built snowmen. They visited the horses to feed them treats. The whole time, Rosalía tried to answer their questions about where their daddy was without crying.

Emma stayed with them at the house. She bustled around cooking, cleaning, caring for the children, and tending to the steady flow of friends and relatives who stopped by. She bravely wore a smile on her drawn face for the twins, but anyone who knew her could see her heart was broken, her pain profound. "I've lost my only child," she lamented. When she and Rosalía crossed paths in the kitchen or the living room, they grasped each other tightly, wordlessly, as if emptying their souls into each other.

Emma doted on her grandchildren more than usual. She read them their favorite books, helped them put together puzzles, bathed them, made cookies. "Pray for your daddy," she said, tucking them into bed and kissing them goodnight. "He's with Jesus now."

Abe's father kept out of sight. His way of dealing with his son's death was to stay home alone, fixing things that didn't need repair, cleaning equipment that was already spotless.

Guapo wandered around the house and yard, whimpering and looking everywhere for Abe. He maintained endless vigils at the head of the driveway, at the door to the master bedroom, by the woodstove in the kitchen where he slept on a ratty, worn out Chimayó blanket. Every time the phone rang, he rushed to it and sat by expectantly with his ears perked up, waiting for Rosalía to pick up the receiver. When he heard a voice on the other end that wasn't Abe's, he flopped down, rested his head on his front paws, and sighed.

Guapo's mourning got to Rosalía. She called Sam. "Please come get this damn dog. He's driving me crazy. I can't stand it."

"What do you want me to do with him?"

"Shoot him. Put him out of his misery. And mine."

"Really? You want me to shoot Guapo?"

"No, of course not. Tie him up, put him in your barn— I don't know. Anything so I don't have his sorrow to deal with in addition to my own."

The day of the funeral was unusually sunny and mild for March in the mountains. Guests parked in the still frozen alfalfa field and walked up the hill to the site of the memorial service, in a grove of bare branched cottonwoods that were beginning to bud. To provide seating, Sam had arranged rows of straw bales in a semicircle, covering them with blankets and tarps. Nearly two hundred of Abe's family, friends, colleagues, and neighbors had assembled on the hilltop. A trio of old-time New Mexican musicians played gentle waltzes. Guests gathered in clusters to talk, while kids ran around, jumping on and off the straw bales, oblivious to the sadness of the occasion.

A hush enveloped the crowd when Rosalía appeared at the bottom of the hill. Her black suede western style coat half open over her pregnant belly, a Stetson low on her brow, and her curly, silky, black hair loose on her shoulders. She walked slowly up the incline, leading Abe's beloved appaloosa, Chocolate. The horse pranced nervously, his four white feet dancing as he shook his long, flowing mane and whisked his tail across his spotted white rump. Grandpa Nez's beautiful stamped silver headstall and the silver trim on the empty saddle glinted in the noontime sun. In the stirrups, Abe's tall dress boots, polished to a gleaming mahogany, faced backward. As Rosalía reached the top of the hill, her children ran from their grandmother's side to grasp their mother around the knees. Sam took the reins from her and looped them over a low hanging branch.

Suddenly Guapo appeared. As if on command, he sprang onto the horse's back and settled himself behind the saddle.

Sam leaned closer to Rosalía and whispered. "I don't know how he got loose. I had him chained up good."

"It's OK," she said. "As long as he behaves."

One after another, Abe's friends and family stepped forward to talk about his kindness or special things he'd done for them. A few told stories—how mischievous he was as a kid, the practical jokes he played on his friends. Some read poems they'd written in his memory or recited from Abe's favorite poet, Emily Dickinson.

Father José, the priest who had married Abe and Rosalía in the apple orchard, stood beside the casket and read aloud from a prayer book in his deep, mellow, Spanish accent. Guapo whimpered, leapt down from Chocolate's back, and nervously threaded his way in and out of the gathering, sniffing at pant legs, skirts, and boots. Gradually, the crowd began to notice him. He paused and then raised his muzzle to the breeze as if searching it for a particular scent. When the dog approached the casket, Father José looked up from his Psalter and halted in midsentence. Guapo sniffed along the edge of the coffin lid, threw back his head, and howled a series of eerie, otherworldly wails that raised the hair on Rosalía's arms. She closed her eyes and bowed her head as the other mourners shifted uncomfortably in place. Sam made a grab for Guapo's collar, but the dog deftly eluded the cowboy's hand, turned his back on the assembly, and trotted purposefully down the hill. To everyone's astonishment, Rosalía jerked Chocolate's reins loose from the branch and vaulted onto his back. She kicked her husband's boots out of the stirrups, and spurred the startled horse after the dog. Guapo saw her coming after him. He took off at a dead run, heading for the highway. She leaned over the horse's neck, urging him into a full gallop, angrily yelling through his wind whipped mane, "You come back here, Guapo, you goddamn dog! Don't you dare do this to me. Come by! Heel!"

Rosalía was gaining on him and reaching for her lariat.

Guapo paused at the edge of the highway and looked back, then ran at top speed onto Route 96, heading straight for a lumber truck that was barreling down the road with a full load of ponderosa logs.

Rosalía reined the horse to a halt when she reached the road and screamed after the dog. "I am not gonna put you back together this time, you sonofabitch! You hear me?"

The driver swerved as much as he could to avoid hitting Guapo, but it was no use. Rosalía knew he couldn't risk overturning his load by braking suddenly. She covered her eyes with a gloved hand, waiting for the inevitable thud.

The truck driver downshifted, his engine roaring in protest. He came to a stop a hundred feet past the entrance to the driveway. Leaping down from his rig, he ran back toward Rosalía, who sat motionless, her hands crossed on the saddle horn, her brimming eyes staring vacantly out over the mesas.

"Ma'am," the driver gasped, "was that your dog? I'm so sorry! I did what I could to avoid him, but with them logs, I really couldn't get out of his way. He was making a beeline straight for my bumper."

"I know it wasn't your fault," Rosalía said, huge tears streaming down her face. "He was my husband's dog. We're having his funeral right now up on the hill. I guess now we're burying both of them today."

"I am so sorry for your loss, Ma'am. You're Abe Garcia's wife, no? I heard about that accident. I am so, so sorry. Everybody thought highly of your husband."

Sam ran up, his chest heaving as he panted for air.

Rosalía pulled Abe's Winchester out of its scabbard on

the side of the saddle and handed it to Sam. "Would you go find Guapo? He's probably dead in the ditch across the road. But if that damn dog's not dead, by God, shoot him. And this time I mean it."

She turned to the truck driver and wiped the moisture from her face. "Thank you for stopping. Please don't blame yourself. It was the dog's fault, not yours. I don't hold you responsible in the least. My family and I appreciate your kind thoughts. Thank you."

She wheeled the horse around and loped back up the hill to the funeral.

The pallbearers were lowering Abe's casket into the freshly dug grave beneath the cottonwoods when Sam appeared, carrying the dead dog wrapped in his tattered Chimayó blanket. The cowboy's leathery cheeks glistened as he gently laid the bundle on top of the coffin, rose, and slowly ambled away.

The guests walked down to the house after the burial and sat at picnic tables fashioned out of planks and sawhorses, with boards across stumps for benches. People had brought generous quantities of homemade food: tamales, green chile stew, tortillas, venison and elk roasts, casseroles, desserts. When Rosalía noticed some of the men wandering off, probably for a pull on a whiskey bottle or a toke of marijuana, she took Sam aside. "Please make damn sure nobody drives home drunk or stoned. We don't need anymore highway carnage. Take their keys away from them if you have to."

When the last of the guests left, the sun was red as a thermometer bulb descending through an orange sky toward the horizon of angled mesas now turning black and opaque. The house grew chilly. Rosalía stoked the fire in the living room fireplace and then settled into the couch that faced it, a twin on each side of her. She put her arms around their tiny shoulders, pulled them to her, and nuzzled the tops of their heads, Mattie's hair thick, straight, and shiny black like his father's; Chela's hair fine, dark, satiny, and wavy like her own.

"Mommy?" Chela asked. "Are we ever gonna see Daddy again? Ama says he's gone to heaven to be with Jesus."

"We'll see him in our dreams, darlin'. Don't you ever forget that he loved you and Mattie more than anything else in the whole world. He thought the sun rose and set on your beautiful heads, and so do I."

"Then why'd he go away?" Mattie asked.

Rosalía drew her son closer. "He didn't go away because he wanted to. It was just something that happened, something awful. The man driving the truck behind him couldn't stop and ran into your daddy's car. He died, too. His kids and wife miss him as much as we miss your daddy."

She held her children and gazed into the fire, wishing its heat could dry her eyes and warm her soul.

"Mommy?" Mattie asked. "What happened to Guapo?"

Rosalía could barely breathe, her heart impossibly heavy, an iron ingot dropping to the bottom of a deep pool.

Before she could answer, Chela said: "I know! Guapo

went to be with Daddy, so he won't be so lonely over there in heaven without us."

Rosalía squeezed her children. "I think that's exactly what happened, honey. I'm sure they're together."

Under her breath, masked by the sound of crackling and popping as the logs shed sparks, she added, "The bastards."

7

Granny

Jimbo Lewis sat in his 1978 MGB where it had rolled to a stop on the gravel shoulder off a New Mexico road. He figured he was southwest of Deming and Interstate 10 near the Mexican border. A cloud of steam billowed from under the hood, obscuring the front end of his car, and the needle on the temperature gauge shot past the H.

He had no idea how cars worked, but looking at the engine seemed to be the guy thing to do. He popped the hood and got out of the car. Like a rattlesnake, the overheated engine's persistent hissing warned him to keep a healthy distance. Could the sucker explode? Jimbo wondered. He studied the smoking beast and ran a hand through his thick, rumpled blond hair. "Shit," he said. When the smoke and sizzle diminished somewhat, he cautiously stepped closer to eyeball the engine. Unfortunately, no sign on any valve or belt or gizmo conveniently announced "shot transmission" or "broken radiator."

On both sides of the road that meandered along the border, the flat, bare, dirt brown landscape reminded him of toast. "Toast," he mumbled. "Yeah, that's what this place is like—dry, crusty, burned toast. Damn! I never should have left the interstate."

He fervently hoped a Good Samaritan with excellent mechanical skills and a set of metric tools would happen by, but he knew that was unlikely. Drivers of the few cars and trucks that passed by at warp speed barely turned their heads his way. He could almost hear them: "Huh, college boy's toy foreign car blew up. Fuck 'im."

The August afternoon was scorching hot, triple digit temperatures baking the asphalt, sending shimmering waves of heat into the air, blurring the watery lines between earth and sky. Standing in the searing sun in his Madras plaid Bermudas, pink polo shirt, and flip-flops beside his busted car, Jimbo felt like his brains were roasting. His eyes, too. Muttering a few more expletives, he put on a bill cap, locked the car as much as you can lock a ragtop with major holes in its fabric and a cracked rear window, and walked back to the nearest settlement, the six trailer, fifty junked car town he'd passed a few minutes ago.

It had all gone bad so fast. There he was, merrily tooling down the two-lane road in his beloved, if battered, sports car, humming along with the Beach Boys tune on his Walkman, heading toward a bright, post-graduation future in California, where he'd open a bar on the beach or a recording studio or a surf shop or something. He could always pour drinks, wait tables, or pound nails while waiting for something better to come along. Then, in the middle of "Little Deuce Coupe," the engine blew.

Jimbo trudged past a faded sign that said "Los López, New Mexico, Population 58." The deserted downtown appeared to consist of a few old boarded-up brick buildings. A sign on the first one said "Garza's De Soto-Nash Rambler Dealership" in faint letters. Across the street was a movie theater, whose broken marquee read "Singing in the Rain," with half the letters missing. The side of the last building that Jimbo went by advertised brands that had mostly disappeared long ago: Fleer's Double Bubble bubblegum, O-So-Grape soda, Kelvinator appliances.

As bleak as things looked, Jimbo firmly trusted he'd somehow be able to get his car fixed and soon be on his way west again. A minor setback like this wasn't enough to make him rue his decision to leave town after graduation: Ohio State, history major, Spanish minor. He had no money, of course, and his father had cut up his credit cards. His California dreams were vague at best—he'd never been there. But he knew for certain he wanted out of Columbus and the Midwest's bone numbing winters and sultry summers, and away from his overbearing father who'd never said a kind word to him in his life. He also was putting a little distance between himself and Chelsea, his sweet but ditsy girlfriend, who desperately wanted him to marry her in a big, splashy wedding. "We'll have eight bridesmaids," she told him. "And a pink and black color scheme."

The future she dangled in front of him like her unhooked Wonderbra involved helping run her mother's hair salon, maybe turn it into a day spa. Like many an itchy-footed young man during the last two hundred years of American history, when things got complicated on the home front, Jimbo headed west.

On the far side of Los López, Jimbo found a business that was open, a shabby Dairy Queen. A teenage waitress watched him walk toward the drive-up window, her elbows on the counter, the screen pulled shut to keep out the flies. She was cracking gum loudly and desperately, as if she needed to break the silence of this desolate place.

Her penciled on eyebrows drooped, she frowned empathetically, and gave him the bad news: there was no garage before Lordsburg, sixty miles west, almost on the Arizona state line. "Or you can go back to Deming," she said, crack, crack, pop.

"Are there any mechanics around here?" Jimbo asked in a tired, plaintive voice.

"There's Jesús Díaz, " she said, snap, snap. "His trailer's the orange and turquoise one behind the water tower." She pointed south.

"Is he a decent mechanic?" Jimbo asked.

She shrugged, snap, whoosh, pop. "They say so. If he ain't drunk."

"Does he have a phone?"

"Doubt it," chomp, chomp. "He don't pay his bills."

The trailer looked to be about a mile away, a beat to shit, blue '72 Chevy pickup parked next to it. Jimbo didn't want to walk in that heat for nothing. "Do you think he'll be home now?" he asked.

"Yup," she said, snap, crackle, snap, snap, whoosh, pop. "The bar ain't open yet."

When Jimbo knocked on the trailer's aluminum siding, a man he assumed to be Jesús came to the door in a once red T-shirt and jeans bleached nearly white from repeated washings and an overdose of Clorox. He was probably twenty eight but looked fifty five. He was barefoot; his toes were hairy. A half empty beer bottle hung from his hand like a deflated party balloon.

"¿Qué quiere?" he said gruffly, resting his arm lazily against the frame of the torn screen door. He hadn't shaved in days. Jimbo thought the man's eyes looked like a pair of black olives swimming in chorizo grease. A big gut hung over a tightly cinched belt that kept his jeans from sliding down his narrow hips and skinny legs.

In a fumbling mixture of English and C+ university Spanish, Jimbo told him his "carro" was "roto."

Jimbo quickly discovered not even lizards move after 9 a.m. during a southwestern New Mexican summer. Jesús certainly didn't. "Too hot now. We get your car mañana," he said.

Jesús picked Jimbo up the next morning at the roachy, musty local Motel Two, where he'd spent a rough night drinking beer, eating a rubbery DQ burger and cold, soggy fries while watching amazingly stupid, snowy, jittery TV reality shows on a circa 1965 black and white idiot box. They hauled his car back to Jesús' trailer with a chain, no tow bar. Jimbo was pissed off. His lovely wire spoke hub-caps, his cheap but serviceable Kenwood stereo, the car radio, and, dammit, his Frisbee, had disappeared over-night. Fortunately, the thieves hadn't bothered to steal his balding tires or worn clothes.

Jesús immediately diagnosed the problem as a busted water pump. Said he'd have to get a part from El Paso, and could Jimbo front him twenty bucks? Then he announced he was quitting for the day. "How about a beer?" he asked.

"Uh, it's a little early for me," Jimbo said. "I don't usually drink before, oh, say ten in the morning."

"You a college boy?" Jesús slurred the words and screwed up his ruddy, bristled face to check out the young Anglo.

Jimbo could see Jesús was already pretty drunk. "Yeah. I graduated a couple of months ago. I'm heading for California."

"The local school's lookin' for a fourth-grade teacher. Classes are starting, and we don't got one. Y'interested?"

"What happened to the regular teacher?"

Jesús smiled. "See, Mrs. McCarthy, the widow lady who's taught fourth grade since I went there? She got herself knocked up and left town pretty quick last week. She was 54."

"I don't have a teaching certificate," Jimbo said.

"Don't matter. Don't none of them teachers got the right papers, I'll betcha."

"I doubt I'm cut out for teaching. But thanks."

In the two weeks it took for the part to arrive from El Paso—Jimbo could have walked there faster—he and Jesús drank up Jimbo's spare change. So the water pump went back to El Paso, and Jimbo decided to take the teaching job after all. What the hell. As soon as he got a little ahead in his finances, he could reorder the part and head for California in his bare rimmed, radioless MGB.

Probably 70 percent of the kids in Jimbo's cement block, tin roofed classroom were from the other side of the border, Los López's twin city of El Molinillo. This was in the mid '90s, when borders were still fluid, people meandered back and forth like birds and butterflies, and school kids weren't yet the enemy. Coming from the overfed Midwest, he was shocked to realize that for a lot of the kids, the school lunch program provided their only reliable meal of the day.

Many students' school attendance had been irregular at best. A few couldn't even read. Jimbo talked to the school librarian, Mrs. Padilla. She was a kind hearted volunteer in her mid-seventies who drove into town every day from her ranch. "I'll get some bilingual children's books. They'll be easier and more relevant to the kids than the school texts," she said.

He suspected she bought them with her own money.

Jesús's sons, Chepo and Memo, and Mrs. Padilla's granddaughter, Lucy, could read fairly well. To keep them occupied, Jimbo assigned them to help the slower readers.

Chepo and Memo weren't twins, but with their nearly identical thick, straight, black hair, round, brown faces, and lean bodies, they were obviously brothers. They also had the same spirited, impish gleam in their black eyes that told their novice fourth grade teacher he'd better be on his toes and not turn his back on them if he could help it. He never knew what tricks they'd have up the missing sleeves of their cutoff T-shirts. Chepo, the older one, was the ringleader. Memo was his brother's straight man. They kept the classroom in a constant state of uproar with their corny, bilingual jokes that Jimbo never understood, their merciless teasing of the girls, and their spitballs when the teacher was busy at the blackboard.

Shortly after Jimbo started teaching, the principal, Mr. Gallardo, stalked into Jimbo's classroom. He had just made a few announcements over the antiquated PA system. "What's going on in here?" he asked angrily.

The fourth-graders tittered. The principal silenced them with an evil look.

Jimbo stammered. "I ... I'm putting our spelling words on the blackboard. Why? Is something wrong?"

"Boy, you need to get a handle on these mule headed Mescans!" Mr. Gallardo barked. "One of 'em musta shot a spitball at the loudspeaker, and it damn near busted my eardrums. You give 'em an inch, they'll take your foot."

The kids turned to stare at Chepo. His eyes were wide with innocence, but after the principal stormed out of the classroom, Jimbo saw the slightest smile cross his lips.

Around Los López, people mostly spoke Spanish, including the Anglo minority. Jimbo quickly found out precisely how bad his command of the language was. Especially in the beginning, he couldn't understand a word anybody was saying to him, even when they spoke slowly for his benefit. Their brand of castellano bore little resemblance to the academic language he'd (sort of) learned in college.

He and his students fumbled along, through math, English, geography, the basic fourth grade stuff, the teacher with his Spanish/English dictionary at hand. Kids like Chepo, Memo, and Lucy, who were fluent in both languages, frequently served as his translators.

In addition to teaching him words and expressions that weren't in the dictionary, his pupils were also his cultural informants.

"Dogs turn into witches at night," Memo solemnly told him.

"You'll get sick if you drink a cold Pepsi while you're ironing your shirts," one of the girls said.

"There's onzas and simurgos and chupacabras around here," Chepo warned.

Sipping a beer with Jesús after school one day, Jimbo asked him why Chepo and Memo, who were a year and a half apart, were both in the fourth grade.

"Their mother took 'em with her to Chihuahua a couple years back after we broke up, and they missed a lot of school while they was there, Chepo especially, when he got hepatitis. She gave 'em back to me last year, said her new boyfriend didn't want 'em around, another man's kids. You let me know if they cause trouble. I'll whup their butts."

Even if they did misbehave, Jimbo wasn't going to tell Jesús. He liked the boys. They were smart, they were quick learners, and once they started to work with the slower kids, they quit picking on them.

Chepo was the class clown. "I'm going to be a magician—or maybe a psychic," he told Jimbo. With money he made sweeping out the little grocery store in town, he sent away for sleight-of-hand gear: magic wands, disappearing coins, trick playing cards with extra aces. Mrs. Padilla got him books on magic and biographies of famous magicians like Houdini and psychics like Uri Geller. Try as hard as he might, Chepo never mastered the art of bending spoons. The cheap metal cutlery in the cafeteria was all crooked, but nobody believed he had bent those spoons with his extraordinary mental powers.

One day, the boys weren't in school. It was unusual; they rarely missed class, and never unless they were sick. When they didn't show up for the third day in a row, Jimbo rode his bike to Jesús's trailer after school. The truck was gone, and he wasn't home.

Jimbo noticed Jesús's rotund neighbor, Mrs. Jiménez, an infamous mitotera—a gossip—sitting placidly on the stoop of her trailer like Jabba the Hutt. "¿Jesús no está en casa?" he asked her.

"Jesús gone to Las Cruces with the kids," she said in her toothless, barely understandable English.

Jimbo was annoyed. "Why didn't he tell me?" he groused to himself.

Mrs. Jiménez slyly eyed the tall, clean-cut güero. "They get into trouble over there in México. Jesús decide to get them outta town for a while."

"What kind of trouble?" Jimbo asked, wondering what sort of serious mischief an eleven year old and a ten year old could get up to, especially in a small town in Mexico, where the law was far more forgiving than on the US side of the border.

Her face lit up in a smile that was all gums save her single snaggletooth, Mrs. Jiménez invited him into her trailer for a beer; there was no room for both of them on the flimsy, aluminum steps she fully occupied. Inside, Jimbo perched on the edge of her sticky, plastic covered sofa and twisted the cap off a Bud Lite.

"The cops have their grandmother in jail there, and the boys decide to bust her out," Mrs. Jiménez said, taking a swig from her beer bottle.

"What?"

"They have a gun," she told him with a conspiratorial leer.

"Where'd they get a gun?"

"Jesús have an old .22 rifle. Use to hunt rabbits and snakes with it—for meat, y'know."

"So they held up the jail at gunpoint? My God."

Mrs. Jiménez laughed, jiggling the rolls of fat under her chin, on her chest, her belly, her tree-trunk thighs, and above her elbows. "They try to. The chota, he have drink a bottle of sotol, but still he grab the barrel and get the gun away from the boys pretty quick. It not even loaded. Then he try to chase them out.

"Chepo," she said, still chuckling with every one of her fat cells, "he see a dust devil come down the street head directly for the jailhouse, but the chota, he have his back turn to the door and don't see it. It was a good size one, spinning like crazy, scare the dogs, throw trash and dirt and chickens around. So strong it knock over a farm wagon.

"'You better let my grandma outta here right now!' Chepo yell. 'I mean it!'"

"'Yeah?' The drunk chota say. 'What you gonna do about it, escuintle?'

"'I'm a magician, and I'm gonna send a tornado to get you if you don't open that cell door, ya mismo!' Chepo holler. Then he start making woo-woo sounds, and he wave his arms, and he talk lotsa kinds of make up mumbo jumbo words.

"The chota begin to laugh the kid off, then he see the dust devil head straight for him. He throw the keys at Chepo and take off out of the calabozo like La Llorona herself is after him. Hee, hee!" Mrs. Jiménez laughed. Tears were streaking her plump, pink cheeks. "I think I'm gonna wet my pants."

"So did they get their granny out of jail?" Jimbo asked, visualizing his prize pupils hustling a tottery, gray haired crone in a flour sack dress out of a cell and across the border half a block down the street.

"¡Sí, señor! When Jesús find out, he put everybody in the pickup, and they head for Cruces. He have a brother lives there."

Chepo and Memo were back in school the following week, grinning like they'd won the Super Bowl, their pals clapping them on the back. Jimbo kept them after school. "I heard about you busting your granny out of jail in Mexico," he said solemnly.

The boys beamed.

"Wasn't there any other way of handling the situation?" he asked in a fatherly, Anglo tone.

"No," Chepo said. "They put her in there because her

boyfriend—well, he's her ex-boyfriend now—was muling meth across the border, and he didn't pay off the Molinillo cops. She didn't do nothing wrong."

"Anything," Jimbo said. 'She didn't do *anything* wrong."

"Right," Chepo said with a big grin.

"You should meet our granny," Memo piped up. "She's real nice."

That weekend Jimbo went to see if Jesús was making progress on his car. Now that he had income from the teaching job, he'd been able to pay for the new water pump. Jesús claimed he was working steadily on the MGB, tuning it up, installing the pump, getting the car ready for the trip to California.

Jesús was sitting in a plastic lawn chair. Jimbo greeted the mechanic with one of those complicated bro handshakes he had finally mastered with a little help from Chepo and by practicing in front of a mirror. "What's the qué pasó, dude?" he asked, planning to slowly get around to the topic of the boys' jailbreak.

The screen door creaked open, and a striking woman Jimbo had never seen before sauntered out of the trailer. She must have been at least forty five, but she didn't seem much older than Jesús. New girlfriend? Jimbo wondered. She stood on the top step in red patent leather wedgies. Firm, brown breasts crested the edge of her tight, black knit tube top like twin moons on the rise, and her abundant raven hair cascaded down her shoulders in thick, wavy tresses. She flashed Jimbo a million dollar smile and managed to shove her long fingers into the back pockets of toreador pants that clung to her hourglass figure like an extra layer of skin. In a honeyed voice, she said: "Hi. You must be my grandsons' teacher."

"Granny" was the reason Jimbo stayed in Los López for another year and a half.

GLOSSARY

abogado/a   attorney

abuelito   diminuitive of abuelo, grandfather

"Ay te watcho."   New Mexican Spanglish expression meaning, "Be seeing you."

befreundet   in German, to be friends and/or romantically linked

buena idea   good idea

cabrón   cuckold; literally, billy goat

calabozo   jail, cell, dungeon; origin of calaboose

camposanto   graveyard, cemetery

carnal, carnales   flesh and blood, brother/s

carne adovada   usually pork cubes marinated in red chile sauce, then cooked very slowly

"Carro . . . roto."   "Car . . . broken."

castellano   Castilian, the Spanish language

chamacos   kids

chamisa/ **chamiza**	rabbit brush, related to sagebrush
chica	girl
chota	cop, policeman
chupacabra	literally, goat-sucker; a blood-sucking cryptid said to prey on goats (cabras), sheep, and possibly humans
churros	fritters, ridged lengths of doughnut-like deep fried pastry
cuete	handgun, pistol
curandera	folk healer
documento	document
ejido	communal land originally granted to New Mexico settlers by the Spanish crown
el mismo	the same, the very one
empanadas	half-round filled turnovers, usually baked
escuintle/ **escuincle**	brat, kid; in Náhuatl, literally, dog
"Está chingado."	"It's fucked up."
Frijolitos Pintos	(a nonsense song popular in New Mexico)

Little pinto beans, purple carnations,
Oh, how they suffer, those who are in love.

Pretty little mamma, here comes Vincent.
Pull him out a bench, so he can have a seat.

He caught the chicken pox, he caught measles,
Leaving his face looking like fried pork rind.

Here is my mother-in-law, coming down the hill.
She jumps over the woodpile, and does a somersault.

A spotted dog, spotted and big-eared,
Searches for her tail, but finds it has been bobbed.

gran pecado	a serious sin
guapo	handsome, brave, bold
güero/a	a light-skinned and/or blond person
hermanos	brothers
hijo	son
hogan	a traditional one-room Navajo dwelling, usually made of timbers and mud wattle, with a single doorway facing east
hombre	man
huevos	literally eggs or testicles; figuratively nerve, audacity, courage, balls
huevos rancheros	an egg dish in the Southwest and Mexico, usually a corn tortilla topped with a fried egg, salsa and cheese
jefe/a	boss; chief
"¿Jesús no está en casa?"	"Jesús isn't home?"
La Llorona	the ghost of a woman who wanders in the night weeping and searching for the children she drowned
locos	crazies
malcriado	spoiled; badly brought up

matanza	in New Mexico, a communal butchering
mecánico	mechanic
"Mejor sola que mal acompañada."	"You're better off on your own than in bad company."
mi amor	my love, my dear
mitotero/a	a gossip, a rumor-monger
mojados	literally, wetbacks; a deprecatory term for illegal migrants
"No sabemos."	"We don't know."
onza	in northern Mexico, a variety of wildcat or puma
patas arriba	paws up; upside down or dead
pendejo	fool; literally, pubic hair
primos	cousins
"¿Qué crees?"	"Guess what?" "What do you think?"
"Qué en paz descanse."	"May he/she rest in peace."
"¿Qué pasa?"	"What's up?"
"¿Qué quiere?"	"What do you want?"
"¿Qué tiene?"	"What does it have?" "What's wrong with it?"
ranchera	a type of traditional music popular in rural northern Mexico and the Southwest US

ranfla	in parts of New Mexico and Mexico, slang for car; possibly derived from Rambler, a make of American automobile
sauer	German for sour, but can also mean bad tempered, cranky
simurgo	a mythical flying creature mentioned by Borges, Bolaño
sotol	an intoxicating liquor made from a variety of maguey; a popular drink in northern Mexico, especially in Chihuahua state
stuffed sopaipilla	a large fritter, usually filled with meat, onions, chile, lettuce, tomato, and cheese. Similar to a Navajo taco
"Suerte, hermanos."	"Good luck, guys."
tía	aunt
tío	uncle
troca	truck
vato	dude, guy
vigas	roof beams; in New Mexico, typically peeled pine logs
"What's the qué pasó?"	"What's happening?" "What's up?"
ya mismo	right now

ACKNOWLEDGMENTS

First of all, thanks to my sister, Polly Arango, for introducing me to New Mexico. Life has not been the same since she invited me to Taos at Thanksgiving in 1963. I can still recall the fabulous feast as well as the magical scent of piñón in that clear mountain air.

Picking the brains of knowledgeable persons is a fascinating aspect of writing. Thanks to the following people who have been generous with their know-how.

Although vehicles are a leitmotif in this collection of tales, they defy my comprehension. Jeff Benson and Gordon Self from Performance Imports in Albuquerque were helpful in this realm, as were my car savvy neighbors, Joe Shea and Roy Pendelton.

My brother Dick Egan is so old he remembers Nash Ramblers and other disappeared brands mentioned in *Granny*. Another Egan bro, Patrick, imparted a thing or two about duck hunting and how to serve up the birds. John Arango contributed to my understanding of legal matters.

Nobody knows Albuquerque's La Luz Trail like David Hammack, and I am thankful to him for providing descriptions that saved me a hike up the mountain for *Time Circles*. Dr. Jim Findlay and Dr. Maggie Werner-Washburn's knowledge of New Mexico's birds and plants served me well.

Mahina Drees and Barney Burns shared their familiarity with northern Mexico, especially the hootch.

Thanks to Noël Bennett and Kathy Chilton who remembered details for me of Navajo life and ceremonials. Pediatrician Lance Chilton supplied the proper formula for the 1920s infant in *Green Eyes*. Anna Masterson provided a vet tech's expertise for *Guapo*; our talented buddy Spud provided the inspiration.

Jack Loeffler graciously allowed me to lift an Edward Abbey quote from his book, *Adventures with Ed: A Portrait of Abbey* (University of New Mexico Press, 2002).

Thanks to Linda Escobar for permission to quote her lyrics to "Frijolitos Pintos" in *Guapo*.

Special thanks to Bob Schacochis, who steered me in the right direction with an early version of *Carnales* and with my writing in general, urging me to cut loose.

In hopes of getting the New Mexican Spanish right, I relied on María del Rosario Fiallos, Bennett Hammer, Juan Cabrero-Oliver, Fernando Mayans, Bernadette Caraveo, and *A Dictionary of New Mexico and Southern Colorado Spanish* by Dr. Rubén Cobos.

Reading a story aloud to someone helps a writer find and repair clunks and clotted sentences. Teal McKibben, a longtime inspiration and pal, listened to early drafts of these stories. She wasn't shy about telling me what she thought of my tales—or about anything else, for that matter. She is now deceased and ever to be missed.

The transformation of a manuscript into a book is a task not unlike taking a pantry full of ingredients, including many of less than optimum quality, and converting them into a savory potage. With Editor & Chief of Papalote Press, Carol Eastes, I cut, chopped, stirred, seasoned, and deglazed this manuscript. Additional editing was provided by Cinny Green and Pat Reed.

The author photograph by María del Pilar Arango makes me look better than I actually do. Assistance in finding the right cover art came from photography galleries Scheinbaum & Russek, Ltd. and Verve Fine Art.

Special thanks to Alex Harris for the use of his terrific photograph *Black Mesa, New Mexico, looking east from Fred Cata's 1957 Chevrolet Belair, July 1987* from his wonderful book, *Red White and Blue and God Bless You* (University of New Mexico Press, 1992).

Heaps of praise, as always, to Barbara Haines for her design of *La Ranfla* and all my fiction books.

Thanks to our publicist, Michael Hice, for attempting to make me famous.

To the Pachamamas, my wonderful helpmates, many thanks for your years of loyalty and reliability that have freed me up to keep the store going while I worked on my books: Lolly Martin, Donna Herring, Mary Berkeley, and Bill Farmer.

To my family and friends (including Frank Aon), ¡muchísimas gracias a todos!

Martha Egan

ABOUT THE AUTHOR

"I always intended to get serious about writing fiction at some point," says author Martha Egan. "But it took a hideous experience with US Customs to force me into it." The result was a semi-autobiographical novel, *Clearing Customs*, named Fiction Book of the Year for 2005 by *OnLine Review of Books & Current Affairs*. Her next novel, *Coyota*, won a Bronze Ippy Award for Mountain-West Best Regional Fiction in 2008 from the Independent Publishers Association.

Martha Egan has been an importer and dealer of Latin American folk art since 1974 through her gallery, Pachamama, in Santa Fe. The Museum of New Mexico Press published her non-fiction books, *Milagros: Votive Offerings from the Americas* (1991) and *Relicarios: Devotional Miniatures from the Americas* (1994). Since 1991, she has held the honorary position of Research Associate of the Museum of International Folk Art in Santa Fe. In 2004, she was the first recipient of the Van Deren Coke Award from the Friends of Latin American Folk Art.

She holds a BA in Latin American History from the University of the Americas in Mexico City and was a Peace Corps volunteer in Venezuela in the late 60s.

Egan volunteers with the Corrales Residents for Clean Air and Water, the International Folk Art Market, and hangs out with forty-three nieces and nephews. She grew up in northeastern Wisconsin and is a rabid Packer fan.

Papalote Press

Design: Barbara Haines
Text: Hoefler & Frere-Jones Mercury Text G1
Display: Magneto, Interstate, Sultan
Printing and Binding: Maple-Vail Book Manufacturing, Inc.